Sarah, to
God keeps Dra
promises
close to Him &
He will draw
close to you.
Be blessed!
:)
Karen
9-20-18

A Books-A-Daisy® Book

Published by Books-A-Daisy® LLC, May 2012

ISBN 978-1-938678-01-1

A product from the United States of America.

Visit us on the web at www.books-a-daisy.com

~Acknowledgments~

Thank you, first, to God for His many blessings! The biggest of which, his son Jesus Christ.

The next biggest thanks goes out to my hubby. This book wouldn't have been complete, if not for the loving support of my beloved husband, Trenton Graham. Thank you for the tireless hours of listening to my endless stream of ideas, laments, frustrations and breakthroughs. I appreciate you reading excerpts and rewrites and helping me tweak my way to a final product. But most importantly, thanks for always believing in me! God continues to bless me with the best husband and best friend any woman could hope to have.

Special thanks goes to my mom, Regina Eick. She truly spent hours finding and editing those typos my eyes seemed to dance right over, and was instrumental in making those crucial reductions in superfluous detail I found so hard to omit. You were a Godsend, and I can't tell you how much I appreciate your time and encouragement. I'm blessed to have you as my mom.

Finally, one of my biggest inspirations and one of the reasons I started writing in the first place—Karen Caig, English Instructor at University of Arkansas Community College in Morrilton. Never before, and sadly not since, have I met a teacher as amazing as Ms. Caig. She was a mentor and a muse who challenged me and others to reach higher in their creativity, explore literature outside their comfort zone, and personally inspired me to "do something" with my writing. Teachers like her and learning lab instructors like Mr. Todd Rasmussen—who wrote notes of inspiration in my math books to remind me that I could indeed conquer Trig—are incredible people. They leave a lasting impact on the lives of the students lucky enough to have them in their lives. Thanks again, you two. You made one of the most difficult times in my life, one of my fondest. I miss you both.

The Promises You Keep

by

Karen Marie Graham

"I don't care what your thoughts are on the subject, Richard, I simply disagree! The university leaves that decision to my discretion, and I don't agree with you on this anymore today than I did a year ago," said Sydney, fisting her hands in agitation. Doesn't this guy ever quit?

"You haven't been in the teaching world for long, and I'm only trying to help you, Sydney. You need to enforce attendance. It's for their own good! I am not trying to increase your workload. Not that you have much of one, since you don't even vary your course curriculum from one semester to the next," he sneered.

Sydney tried to walk around him, but he stepped in front of her blocking her way.

"I said I won't do that. Responsibility is not defined in your attendance policy. A student is already showing responsibility for improving their lives and minds by completing the work. If a student quits my class, it's by choice. It will not be by force. I won't use an attendance policy to force them to show up every day—one that penalizes them to the point of failure if they don't. You don't consider that in your policy. While thinking you are teaching the younger traditional student the responsibilities of accountability, you end up punishing the older non-traditional student who already knows those responsibilities all too well."

Richard straightened his tie smugly as he glared up at her. "While that may be true, it wouldn't be much of a requirement for a student to attend class if one person could get out of the policy and another can't. It has to be across the board with little exception," Richard swept his hand as if to clear a chessboard of its pieces. "Otherwise, you may inadvertently show favoritism."

"Your rule levied across the board like that is another word for dispassionate. You know as well as I that online and hybrid classes are becoming the norm. Just because this is a small town doesn't mean the newer technologies and ways of doing things won't catch up some day. Your ideas are antiquated, Richard. You just don't want to accept it." She ran her hands through her red hair, and resisted the urge to pull it out.

"Anyway," Sydney continued, trying to skirt around Richard again, "I have things I need to do before school starts tomorrow, and I feel like a broken record saying these things to you again. My decision is made. This subject is closed. I'll appreciate this being the final time we speak of it. Good afternoon, Richard." Finally getting past, Sydney strode purposefully down the hall toward her office.

"I knew if we allowed these hybrid classes that discipline and rigor would soon suffer," called out Richard after her. Getting no reply, he indiscreetly harrumphed and slammed his door.

Sydney sighed. If it weren't enough to still be relatively new to the university she had to go and make an enemy, and with a tenured professor at that. Why can't he let it go? It's been over a year. The larger colleges and universities have online degree programs with no physical classroom required. Richard knows that! Stodgy old man. Why did he keep badgering her?

Smiling to herself she realized that's exactly what he looked like. Throw a pair of Harry Potter glasses on a pot-bellied badger dressed in a three piece suit. Complete the look with a bad comb over, and you'd have Richard. All he needs is a little pocket watch. That thought cheered her up a little as she rounded another corner.

Stopping at the door that belonged to the key in her hand, Sydney sighed. "Professor Sydney Mackenzie, Department of English Literature," announced the brass doorplate in elegant black script. Her office still didn't quite feel like home, if you could call this closet an office, but it worked.

Grabbing her mail from the letter box on her door, Sydney stepped inside and turned on the light, shutting the door behind her. She barely noticed the cheerful bubbly water fountain in the far right corner. She walked blindly by the framed pictures along the wall that held her diplomas and awards. Her feet failed to register the plush faux Oriental rug as she walked around the teakwood desk she'd brought in from home. She absentmindedly laid her laptop, keys, mail, and purse down onto it, and gratefully sank into the leather wingback office chair. She sighed again. Rocking back and forth, Sydney rested her eyes for a moment as she tried to forget about Richard's latest rant.

He was such a jerk. It never failed to amaze her that he just wouldn't let it go. He wasn't even her boss, and the board approved of her—well, most of them did. The only thing she disliked about her job was dealing with Richard.

Thankfully, this would be a short week. Class started in the morning, and tomorrow was a Friday. Thank God! That meant she didn't have to worry about running into Richard as much once school started again. They'd both be too busy with their own course loads for him to ambush her with his opinions.

Sydney was truly glad class was starting again, except for seeing Richard when she couldn't avoid it. Christmas break just about did her in with nothing to work on and no family to celebrate the holidays with. It was going to be great getting back to work first thing in the morning. After tomorrow, she just had to make it through the weekend, and then she could numbly slip back into the routine she loved. She missed her routine.

❧ By the first day of class, the cold weather turned nasty and covered the valley with freezing fog, ice, and snow. After dressing warmly, she headed off to work.

Her short drive to the university provided plenty of time to watch the early morning snow. Big snowflakes cluttered the slate-blue sky as if someone blew from the heavens thousands of those little puffs of dandelions gone to seed. It softly floated down to blanket the layers of ice already present.

Sydney drove to her designated spot in the teachers' garage and parked her car. She paused a few moments and watched as the snow burst gained momentum. There was something fresh, new, and deadly calm about snow and ice she thought.

It fit.

Since David left, Sydney couldn't remember a time when her heart was any less frozen than the ice enshrouding the landscape. Any less beautifully desolate for once having loved someone who was a piece of her soul and then lost him.

David. He was such a loving free-spirit that had blessed and enriched her life. He was mercurial and mischievous—the quintessential melancholy artist who had been her whole world. Who utterly shattered her heart when he left her.

Gone.

She had tried to put that part of her life away, moving as far away from the ghosts of the past as possible. Abandoning her job as a freelance writer, she turned to the quiet routine of teaching at a rural university. Being a writer, she naturally gravitated toward teaching creative writing and composition classes. Helping a beginning writer discover the joys of capturing their ideas and sculpting their thoughts into meaningful works of art helped fill the hollowness of her own creative void.

Work was what she needed most—constant work. Not her freelance writing. It was just too flexible, and not consistent enough to keep her mind occupied full time. She also lacked the motivation to keep herself going, especially where writing was concerned. Writing, for herself or a job, seemed lost to her now. Her mind couldn't focus on the day-to-day demands of massaging a manuscript, sending out the endless queries, and receiving the countless rejections. The last thing she needed right now was another rejection.

She craved a new start, a new job, and a new home. How could she stay in Texas with David's shadow hanging around the house? She couldn't. So running from the shattered ruin she once called her life, she found herself in a new career, buried under work she loved, with no one to answer to, save herself. No spirits walking the corridors of home, office, and her mind. Her memories hadn't haunted her here. Much. The last few semesters had been a blessed blur.

Sydney took one last look at the snow before getting out of the car. David loved the snow. Shaking herself free from the thought, she grabbed her laptop and headed inside—ready to get to work.

~ From a look at the roster, the semester would be very busy. Forty-seven students in all had signed up for this semester's first Creative Writing class. Sydney set out fifty copies of the syllabus on the desk in her classroom knowing full well most didn't bother printing it from her website.

Glancing at the clock on the wall she noted only a few minutes remained before her first class of the day. She was eager to get started.

By 9 o'clock twenty-three of the forty-seven students enrolled showed up. With the weather as nasty as it was, this wasn't surprising. Those that didn't live on or near the campus most likely had played it safe and stayed home, and, unlike Richard, she had the forward thinking policy that attendance wasn't required as long as the work was done. So it made sense many stayed in.

Funny how word got around about things like her lack of an attendance policy. Sydney smiled to herself. It sure would be nice if Richard could overhear a few of the compliments she received. If he could witness how appreciative many of her students were about her class being so flexible. Not that it would probably make much difference with someone as set in his ways as Richard, but the hope was still there that one day he'd see things her way.

Subdued chatter filled the room as the less-than-enthusiastic students waited for class to begin. Conversations bounced around the classroom on topics ranging from how nasty the weather was to forecasts on the difficulties of the coming semester.

"All right, class, let's settle down and get started. My name is Sydney Mackenzie, and I'll be guiding you in exploring the art of creative writing." Sydney picked the syllabi up off her desk and began methodically passing them out to each student as she continued to speak.

"This syllabus, as in each and every class you will ever take from me," she continued, "is your Bible and your salvation. I do not believe in taking attendance." Whoops and clapping erupted. Knowing smiles were passed from those in-the-know to the ones that had thought it was somehow too good to be true— that there was actually such a thing as an in-class class with no attendance policy.

Sydney smiled at the delay and waited until the noise began to die down. "You are expected, present or not, to have each of these assignments completed and turned in on the date indicated. The schedule does not change from what is printed here, so no excuses."

"Even though I don't have an attendance requirement, that doesn't mean I don't want you to come to class." Sydney attempted her most stern teacher-like voice. "I feel a writer is enriched and strengthened by class interaction and discussion. You can almost always count on receiving inspiration on topics to write about when you are in class."

"We critique one another's work, too, helping each other find typos, plot holes, and other opportunities to improve. You'll find that spending time with other writers will help make you a better writer, so all of you are strongly encouraged to be here."

"Also, and I can't stress this enough, pay attention to the due dates. You all have advanced warning, as outlined in the syllabus in your hand, of each and every assignment from now to the last assignment in May. Since there is no attendance requirement, and you have all your work assigned in advance, there are also no excuses for late homework. All reading assignments, tips, examples of student essays, threaded discussions, FAQs, and reference materials are listed there for your convenience. Everything you need to complete your work should you not attend class."

"There are also no tests, as you can see." Another round of applause answered her announcement.

"This means your grade in this class is solely focused on your efforts as a creative writer, and not your ability to match authors' names with their work, memorize publication dates or literary terms. The understanding of those terms will be evinced in your writing itself."

"I'm not expecting Shakespeare or Byron, but I do expect an honest effort."

The kids laughed at the reference.

"If you are weak in this subject then feel free to call upon me in my office during the times denoted on the syllabus. I can also be reached by email. Also, I have a list of personal tutors if you need more help than my schedule allows."

"There is a learning lab, as well. The lab has a full-time instructor named Mr. Rasmussen. You'll find he is very good at critiquing papers, and if you need help in other classes like Algebra, I hear he's a wizard at that, too. The lab's hours of operation and location are also on the syllabus."

"For those who may 'accidentally' lose this syllabus," Sydney waved the papers, "it is available on my home page. Click on the faculty tab at the top of the school homepage to view a list of the professors. Find my name, and click on it."

"No excuses people. On my website, along with the syllabus copy, you will also find links to several writing aid websites, examples of essays, poetry, analytical papers, et cetera, to give you an idea of what each assignments is calling for. Are there any questions?"

A young brunette, dressed more for the ski slopes than for class, raised her hand and tentatively asked, "So, you're saying we don't have to come to class— like ever?"

It was expected. Someone always had to ask.

"Yes, if you're skilled enough to write on your own, and need no conversational inspiration or ideas from your classmates on what to write, then yes, you may just turn in your completed work. Any other questions?"

"What if we're late in turning in an assignment and just can't help it, like a funeral or something?" asked a young man in his late twenties who, by his appearance, looked to be in a punk rock band. "What about that?" No poker face there. He appeared to be mulling over the possibility of using just such an excuse.

Sydney smiled, "Lateness, in general, is not allowed. However, in the case of extreme situations, like the one you mentioned, then that circumstance will be judged individually. Since these assignments are laid out in advance though, and the due dates do not change, there's plenty of time for planning. If you have an unexpected event like a funeral, turn in the work you have, and then come see me. Funerals, for instance, are easy to verify in the newspaper. Funeral home memorial pamphlets are usually plentiful for those who attend." The punk rocker had the grace to look a little discouraged. Sydney hid a smile. Odds are, he'll be very good at writing, but just didn't know it, yet.

"Papers are due every two to three weeks, without fail. If you are ill or must work late unexpectedly, or if your car breaks down on the way to school and you're late to class, you will first need to turn in what you have. Then you will need to provide me with some sort of documentation for the delay, such as a doctor's note, note from a manager or timesheet copy, car repair, or tow bill—you get the idea? Once the emergency is verified, you'll be granted an extension to finish it. Don't misjudge my flexibility. I will not tolerate repeat offenders, and documentation where possible is a must."

"So, what other classes do you teach?" A tiny blonde in a sweater dress, leggings, and UGG boots asked. Her classmates erupted into laughter, all thinking along the same lines.

"Just the classes listed on my home page," said Sydney, smiling at yet another common question. "So now that we know how it works, let's move on."

"The first assignment is an easy one. What I want you to do, without worrying too much about the forms and functions of writing, is to dive right in and write. Brainstorm. Write about a part of you, your life, something about you that you love or hate. Anything that inspires or angers, saddens or delights you about yourself. Write about it."

"Don't write about what you do or want to do, but who you are. This is a great self-discovery exercise, and it's the easiest hundred percent you'll get this semester. Write at least a page and a half, double-spaced, just like it says on the assignment section of the syllabus. Got it?"

The class indicated they understood.

Sydney smiled in anticipation of what looked to be an enjoyable class ahead.

"Good, then I'll expect papers on my desk two weeks from Monday morning. In the meantime, begin to read your first assignment. We'll start discussing it next week."

Sydney knew the same scene would repeat throughout the next few school days as each of her classes had their first official day. Attendance would fall off quickly after that. Most students tested the boundaries of the attendance policy right away, but it usually picked back up around the time the first papers were due. It was then that the fun began.

❧ Snow was still lightly falling as school finished for the day. Thank God for snow tires, Sydney thought.

By the time she got home it was eight degrees. On the drive home the radio weather man announced three inches of snow had fallen since morning. The roads had been cleared before school had ended so the drive was beautiful, and thankfully, uneventful. As she pulled in the driveway, she took a moment to admire her home.

Home was a tongue and groove milled log house nestled in a clearing inside five acres of forest. Beautiful Frazer firs dotted the fence line around her backyard. Towering evergreens surrounded the clearing where her home was cradled. Their broad branches peeked out from under a thin blanket of powdered snow. Douglas fir trees snuggled in among the larger evergreens—each tiny needle pearled with ice. The evergreens softened the stark skeletons of the red maple, pin oak, and river birch glazed gunmetal silver by the ice. The forest hid the cabin from the road and insulated it from the whipping northern winds.

Sydney pressed the garage door opener to open the detached two car garage. She was thankful the person who built the place hadn't ruined the rustic charm of the house by attaching a garage and making it look too modern.

The log home, which she affectionately referred to as her cabin, was crafted entirely of a rich honey-stained cedar, inside and out. The cedar was milled in the D-shaped style, rounded on the outside and flat on the inside, giving the interior walls a smooth finish.

It had a beautiful faux copper roof, with a burnished green patina, that was barely visible from under the thick layer of snow. Two dormers broke through the blanket of white, their shuttered windows overlooking the front yard.

The entire cabin was skirted with a wide covered porch, bordered with rounded cedar columns and hand railings, and accented with black cast iron balusters that glistened with ice. Stacks of firewood lined the south side of the front porch—tucked away from the elements. A wrought iron porch swing hung idle on the other end, waiting patiently underneath its protective vinyl cover for warmer weather, while the hot tub merrily simmered and steamed on the back porch—always ready for a visit.

Sydney found her keys as she headed toward the glass paneled French doors. A soft welcoming glow emanated from the house through panes of sparkling cathedral glass. The whole place was warm, golden and beautiful. Every time she saw it she couldn't help but smile. This was her haven.

Walking in the front door she shook off the snow still clinging to her hair and greeted Baxter, "Hey, boy! How's my good boy today?"

Baxter was a sweet fox hound-beagle mix Sydney had rescued from the local shelter. He greeted her at the door every day, full of life, and lots of wet kisses. He was her best friend, her confidante and the best snuggle-bunny around. The only thing in life she was close to.

Dumping her computer bag on the floor Sydney reached over, patted him on the head, and gave him a light scratch under his chin. "Come on boy, let's light a fire and warm this place up a bit." Baxter ducked his head as he took off in a run, skirting the cordovan leather sofa, barely missing the small oval coffee table, and launched himself into the rocking chair by the fireplace. Sydney couldn't help but laugh, seeing him sitting there thumping his tail madly as the chair gently rocked back and forth from the impact. That silly dog always did seem to understand what she was saying.

Sydney walked toward the fireplace, shedding her coat and laying it on the sofa as she went. She laid her keys and purse on the small entertainment center that sat across from the still moving rocker.

One of the things she first fell in love with about her home was the fireplace. She especially loved building fires in it when winter set in for its long stay. Having lived in the South most of her life, fireplaces had been more ornamental than functional, but farther North they were a necessity, and a welcoming comfort in a frigid world.

The fireplace was designed with smooth river rock. The pale multicolored stones stretched from floor to ceiling. The firebox itself sat two feet off the floor bringing the fire closer to eye level, and making it easier to view when relaxing on the sofa.

The same river rock that encased the chimney and surrounded the fireplace face also created the outer hearth. The hearth rounded out in front of the firebox and created a seating area directly in front of the flames.

Set in the center of the home, it served as a partition that divided the main floor in two. One side of the fireplace housed the living room, kitchen and dining nook. On the other side of the fireplace was the master bedroom and bath. The fireplace was designed with economy in mind. It opened on each side so that the living room and the bedroom shared the warmth and light from a single fire. Because of this, it took six large logs the size of a man's leg to completely fill the cast iron grate inside.

Sydney moved the screen to the side, selected several pieces of wood and added them onto the grate. Lighting a long match, she turned the skeleton key in the rock wall to turn on the gas to help set the logs ablaze. It didn't take long for the fire to catch hold. Tongues of blue and orange greedily curled around the logs as the sap inside began to sizzle and pop. Satisfied the seasoned wood would burn on its own, she turned the gas off and stood for a moment admiring the dancing blues and greens within the growing orange and yellow blaze. So pretty.

Baxter jumped at the back door, begging to go outside. Sydney left the fire to let him out into the backyard. She barely got the door open before he shot out chasing after some unseen target. He ran the perimeter, bouncing through the snow, checking things out—halting here and there, and barking at some unseen intruder. Thankfully, she didn't have to go out with him. When she adopted Baxter from the local shelter she'd had a picket fence installed to keep him safe when he went outside.

Her stomach reminded her that she hadn't eaten much at lunch. Sydney broke off watching the frolicking dog and headed toward the kitchen, picking up her computer bag she'd left by the entry.

The kitchen was open to the living room with only a breakfast bar to separate the two. Along the back wall a stainless steel refrigerator stood next to the matching gas range and microwave. The sink and dishwasher were installed in the breakfast bar. Black Forest Quartz countertops played counter note to the stainless steel. The little flecks of amber in the stone complimented the warm honey tones of the cabinetry and cabin walls. The shiny steel and cold black quartz gave the appearance that a professional chef resided there. Sydney laughed at that. She was no chef.

Placing the computer on the counter, she grabbed a towel from the laundry room in preparation for Baxter's imminent snow covered return. Laying the towel on the barstool she headed back to the side-by-side to grab something to eat for dinner.

Cubed pineapple, sliced strawberries and baby carrots on a bed of spinach made up her main meal—a sprinkle of slivered almonds, and a few wedges of smoked Gouda and mozzarella rounded out the meal quite nicely. A glass of Riesling made the perfect finishing touch. She may not be a chef, but a friend had taught her a little about pairing wine with food. She loved how the crispness of the semi-sweet wine would complement the cheese, bring out the flavors in the salad and echo the tart sugars of the fruit.

Having made her own dinner, Sydney grabbed Bax's food out from under the sink, scooped out his kibble into his dinner bowl and changed out his stale water with fresh. All set there.

Baxter had made quick work of his visit outside and was anxious to be back indoors by the time Sydney had finished. She let him in, dried him off, and then hung the towel over the doorknob for the inevitable next trip outdoors.

Sydney picked up her plate and wine glass and headed through the living room toward the master bedroom. Baxter followed closely in her footsteps hoping for a treat. Baxter loved cheese.

She walked over to the nightstand by the bed and set down her dinner. "Don't even think about it, buster," she warned Baxter.

Grabbing her PJ's from the nearby dresser, Sydney headed for the adjoining bathroom to change. Tossing her work clothes in the hamper, she changed into her flannel pajama bottoms, a loose sweatshirt, and a pair of fuzzy chenille socks.

Picking up her dinner, she returned to the living room to the rocking chair by the fireplace. On the bookshelf lay a new book. Nestling in her oversized rocking chair big enough for two, Sydney settled in for the night with Baxter by her side. Her last thought before diving into her new novel was that Monday morning would come soon enough. She couldn't wait.

⁂ Two weeks had passed since school had started, and the first essays were due. A large stack of papers waited on her desk from the first assignment. The remaining few students that didn't just drop off their papers and leave, were waiting in class, ready to review the reading and discuss any questions they had.

Each of the classes had dwindled down to less than twenty-five students in attendance. Sydney often wondered if that were one of the reasons Richard was such a jerk about her classes. They only *seemed* small in comparison to his; however, the homework, emails, and tutoring never changed from her lack of an attendance policy. In fact, it increased her workload since she ended up repeating answers to questions she'd given in class to those who were absent, but since Richard only taught face-to-face classes, she tried to give him the benefit of the doubt that he just didn't see that her teaching style still required the same, if not more, work as his way of teaching did.

Driving home with a stack of papers and Chinese take-out marked the beginning of the semester routine. She loved her routine. Staggering the due dates of the papers from each of her classes created a manageable, and somewhat constant, workload. Teach class by day, gather papers, pick up gourmet take-out on the way home, eat, grade papers, and jog with Baxter. Toss in a little shopping on the weekend, and some house cleaning, and her schedule was complete. Sydney turned off the main road into her driveway. A fresh set of flurries began just as she caught sight of the cabin.

Glancing at the horizon she noted the evening sky was leaden with the promise of more snow. The glow from the setting sun set the trees to glittering like diamonds in the angle of the waning light.

After entering, Sydney started the fire to warm the place up and let Baxter out to scout the yard for potential invaders. She put out his dinner and refilled the water dish while he hopped around in the snow outside, biting at the falling flakes as if he were snatching insects out of the air.

Sydney changed out of her work clothes and into her jogging suit, while Baxter played. She unpacked her take out dinner and poured a glass of wine. A persistent scratching alerted her that Baxter had finished hunting snowflakes and was ready for some real food. She grabbed his towel to dry him off.

Letting him go off to eat she took her plate and glass and headed for the rocker. No luxury reading tonight, Sydney thought ruefully as she sat down to eat before she began the entertaining, sometimes tedious, process of grading papers. Staring into the fire as she ate, she thought ahead to the essays that awaited her.

The first essay assignments were always the easiest for the student since the author knew the subject matter intimately—themselves. It got the student writing quickly. A kind of a warm up before the real work began. It not only showed her a student's level of writing skill and areas that needed improvement, the papers also allowed her insight into who they really were. She liked that part the best. There were never two students alike, each one was as individual as the snowflakes falling outside.

Getting to know the students as individuals was one reason Sydney didn't teach solely online as some professors in the larger schools chose to do. While online classes serve a valuable purpose for the working adult, as well as easing classroom real estate limitations, there was really nothing that could replace the fun she had in the traditional classroom setting.

Often times the interaction between the different personalities was an important element in sparking creativity. The open, often outspoken students, were instrumental in classroom discussions for getting the shyer students involved in passionate debates. Topics ranging from religion, politics, and personal beliefs were the best to introduce to the talkative ones. She enjoyed playing devil's advocate, too. Many times there was nothing like having a point to defend to get a student interested in writing.

Other advantages to getting to know her students in person meant she could find similarities between stronger and weaker students. This would assist her later in pairing up those who need a little extra help working on their papers. Strong students were invaluable when someone needed help outside her available tutoring hours. It was easier to help them network during class, person-to-person, rather than online.

Finished with her meal, she cleaned up and headed toward the breakfast nook with the papers. The first essay however, was not what Sydney expected.

Self Discovery
Creative Writing
Emily Halliwell

Me

If I were to draw it up for you, use words to describe the ever-changing currents within me, how would you respond? How you see the world is foreign to me. I feel as if I have many selves where the world seems to be made up mostly of one-dimensional people.

There is the daring, soaring brave siren that challenges the world and all in it. She is the one that is whimsical in person, full of the glories of life, living on the intoxication of just being, full of the adventure of discovery, living in the moment, relishing that instant, and daring to do more. She fears nothing— childlike and wondrous. Rapture found in exploring the unknown and I am consumed in the discoveries. Fueled by blind faith in the ability to understand the mysteries, I am rapid in thought, creative in action, flying and soaring above the clouds that for now seem miles below. Unstoppable, irreverent and passionate beyond reason— a free spirit, a fey creature, with laughter in glittering moss green eyes, mischief heard in the lilting voice that changes timbre between low depths of sensuality and the higher pitches of excited bliss— flying, free, unbroken and unfettered. I am like a spirited horse claiming the distance of the plain within seconds and running faster than the wind—happy—wild—carefree.

Then there is the one who is demure, calm, and reconciled to my solitary fate—the one who is content to be alone. Separate. This part of me is centered and craves a world of silence, peace, and quiet reflection. Quiet reflection, wherein I'm forced to contemplate my own mortality— this brief spark of existence which will soon end. I have come to terms with the fact that I am not meant to be long in this world.

The calmer one can go into the depths that few care to face. And in going, travel there quite contentedly and fearlessly. Hearing the darkness calling, sweetly singing its lulling songs of cold and sorrow is like a dark lover calling me home—wrapping its arms about me, lulling me back into its life-less existence. There, whereby its blackness mirrors my own heart's sorrow— it calls me to remember pain, losses, and swallows me up in its cryptic embrace.

The thing that scares others most, like death and dying, scares me least— or at least this side of me. It is an old sensation of knowing what is there—that bleak, all-knowing, sorrowful blackness—and finding comfort in the letting go of caring— the letting go of fighting—gaining the reprieve of giving in. The dark shadow of myself is another part of me. Why should I be afraid?

Only the memory of my family keeps me from wanting to voluntarily embrace the finality of death when that part of me visits the extremes of the mind. In their honor, I struggle on. For now. Soon I will join them. But, not yet. Not yet.

Good Lord, who was this Emily? She writes just like David did. Sydney sat there riveted to her seat unable to tear her eyes away from the paper—no longer seeing the words.

His face, in perfect detailed memory, swam before her eyes. Black wavy hair that was always unkempt, as if any attempt at style was only an afterthought. He kept it long, with wavy locks that threatened to cover his baby blue eyes. That lopsided grin, a product of stitches he'd gotten in a car wreck as a teenager where he learned the hard way to always wear his seatbelt. The angel face of the bastard that had left her. Slamming her pen down Sydney pushed away from the table and paced the room.

The relentless questions that once haunted her came back with slicing clarity. Why did he leave me like that? What was he thinking? How can you love someone then do that to them? Is he happy where he is? Why couldn't he have confided in her? Told her he was unhappy? Worked through the problems with her? Why wasn't she enough to hold on to instead of giving into the ultimate betrayal? Sorrow and rage had finally found her—fresh as the day she'd been left. How dare he shove that knife in her heart, twisting it without a warning, and then leave her to deal with the pain?

She had to get out of the house. She was incapable of staying inside her sanctuary now that the ghost had found her—she had to get out. She had to run. Sydney ripped her vest off the hanger and grabbed her keys. Baxter jumped up and bounded to the back door. He knew that sound.

Sydney tied up her running shoes and snapped Baxter's leash in place. With the park so close and the access roads clear, it was the perfect opportunity to go. Just in time, too. She slammed through the gate, fled into the forest behind her home, down the hidden trail that led her to the park road and away from ghosts of the past.

Glancing at her watch as she began to jog, Sydney noted she had just over an hour before nightfall set in. Thankfully, the flurries had ceased. The pain, however, had not.

~ Who'd have thought she'd have taken up running? After having changed so much in her life, she thought, why not? It seemed after quitting smoking, changing her diet, as well as her location and occupation that she just kept on reinventing herself and trying new things. In the back of her mind she wondered if she were trying to become someone David wouldn't have betrayed. Or maybe she wanted to be someone he wouldn't have loved at all. No, neither thought was exactly the truth. She changed because she needed to be a better person, to take better care of herself, to keep moving forward, to not look back. Of all the new changes, running suited her best, and the state park behind her house was admittedly a glorious place to be indulging in her escape.

When the realtor said the cabin she was to buy backed up to government land she hadn't realized it would be a state park. Maybe she hadn't been listening hard enough. At the time, she just needed to move, and the house was beautiful. Luckily, there was a trail hacked out of the woods, probably by the former owner. It led from her home to the road that circled the park.

It was so easy to get lost in the scenery as she followed the park road. The waning sunlight reflected gold with edges of silver off the icy layers of the trees. The air was clean and brisk, already working its magic as it began clearing away her emotional fog, grounding her to the present, as she put the past both literally and figuratively behind her.

The park was a combination of forest and meadow. It remained mostly a rolling gentle terrain throughout the vast acreage. She had been told there was a lake off somewhere toward the back and a valley a few miles across from the main entrance. It was a wildly popular place for families to camp in the warmer months. Winter, however, left the park mostly to her and the rangers who maintained it.

The snow that blanketed the fields reminded her of a newly ironed sheet—fresh and crisp. It was undisturbed in most places—broken here and there by deer, or by rabbit tracks in others. Baxter could scent the animals Sydney couldn't see and champed at the bit, completely ignoring the scenery, but loving the outing all the same. Given the chance, he'd follow the tracks and run the rabbits or deer to ground. Keeping that in mind, Sydney kept a firm hold on the leash.

She focused on breathing deeply, rhythmically, and settled into the run.

When she'd first started running, breathing was anything but easy. Being an ex-smoker and completely out of shape made the simple act of breathing during a workout a challenge all by itself. She and David had both smoked. They often thought of quitting, but neither had the motivation. David joked they were all going to die someday, right? They both laughed mirthlessly at his morbid sense of humor. Life was what it was, he said, and they went right on smoking.

The day he left her, she found she couldn't even stand the thought of smoking. Her habits were foreign with no one to share them—no sense of camaraderie. Would she have even picked up those habits had she not met David? She'd never know. That part of her life was over, as well.

Her former home became a shell of what it was. It lost its familiar welcome. All her things seemed alien to her without him there, anyway. Something twisted inside her and forced her to change. She sold the home and its furnishings, too.

She no longer loved the city, either, with its busy commutes—compartments within conveyances. Buses, trains, planes, cars all teetered along with their subdued human cargo. No one connecting, just existing, herded from point A to point B to get this and that done. Even when people connected it was digital—artificial. Truncated communication formed in snippets of tweets and posts on social networking sites. The days of sitting at a patio coffee table with a cup of handcrafted coffee and a homemade desert, with people actually chatting one-on-one with a friend, seemed to be a scene from a distant age. It was all so bereft of any humanity, the way she had lived—racing along on a current of purpose driven activities with very few islands of personal connections, other than David.

She wanted a new life. One filled with peace, harmony, communing with nature, to find her center, to be without, and be content. She yearned to live life, not merely exist in a city so modern it'd lost its soul.

Maybe that's why she chose the cabin. She found an earthiness, and a connection with nature there. It was built of nature's bounty itself in its natural form. Unlike the man-made creations of this world, with its synthetic plastics and homes made of particle board, toxic materials, and faux wood, this home was made of strong God-given timber, from a living tree that would someday decay back into the soil, providing a fertile ground for new trees to root and grow.

It still had a soul when she felt like she'd lost hers, lost her way, her place in time—rootless, without family. Perhaps she needed a connection with nature, a permanence, with life going on even while she'd put hers on hold. Not on hold. On hiatus. Until she could heal. She was drawn to the forest, the garden, as if instinctively needing to be where mankind had come from—a paradise to which we all long to return.

Passing by the empty campsites Baxter caught scent of something. He nearly pulled Sydney off the road in his enthusiasm and forced her back to the present. Five years old and that dog still acted like a newly whelped pup. Sydney smiled at him. He loved the two-mile loop they took around the park.

Her jogging course, as she thought of it, began at the back of the park from her exclusive backyard access. She had but to loop through the main entrance, follow the main road to the campground, up the small hill, and back down to the unmarked path home. Not a soul intruded on her thoughts. A rare few camped in the dead of winter. Other than the steady rhythm of her foot falls and Baxter's panting, the forest was quiet. Her thoughts had quieted, as well.

As they rounded the last turn marking the final leg of their run, Baxter came to life again drawing Sydney's attention from the peaceful winter landscape to the comet of fur streaking straight toward them. Looking further ahead, someone was obviously losing the race some distance behind.

Knowing how much "fun" it was to chase down a runaway dog Sydney reduced her speed to a slow walk. She let off the retractable leash and allowed Baxter to change course toward the other pup, just a little bit. She hoped the lure would work, and the other dog wouldn't be able to resist the temptation. Just as she thought, the other canine slowed down to a near stop to warily sniff at them—intending to trot by, no doubt. This gave her the perfect opportunity to grab a hold of its scruff and end its short-lived burst of freedom. Sydney grinned in triumph as her fingers sunk in. "Gotcha!"

Struggling to maintain her balance while crouched down between the two excited dogs, however, made her triumph short-lived. They sniffed and pawed at each other, twisting and turning in an effort to investigate every inch of one another. With tails wagging furiously, neither showed an ounce of menace—or restraint. They acted more like they were the best of friends. They wanted to play, and she was in the way of all that fun!

Thankfully, she only had to endure a couple minutes of their tug-of-war until the runaways' owner arrived in an exhausted fit of heavy breathing.

"You have...."

"no ....i...."

"dea...."

"how grateful ...."

"I am for this," he greeted her while attempting to catch his breath. Leaning over, he braced his hands on his knees.

"So glad...."

"you were here."

"I'm not sure...."

"what I would have done...."

"if you hadn't ...."

"shown up." Kneeling down next to her he relieved her of the wiggle-worm she had been working hard to control.

Sydney answered that it was no problem as she realized he looked familiar. Frowning, she tried to place where she would have seen him before.

Misinterpreting her frown, he continued, "Oh, I'm sorry."

"I'm Brandon...."

"Alexander...."

"You are?"

"Sydney Mackenzie," she returned, as she realized she was certain she knew his face from somewhere. "You look familiar. Have we met somewhere before?"

Brandon, finally getting a good grip on the struggling pooch, took a second look at Sydney.

"Oh, I'm sorry," he continued, having caught his breath.

"I didn't recognize you," he smiled wider in acknowledgement. "We haven't formally met, but we work together at the university. I'm the new Psych professor and school Psychologist. My office is across from Richard's classroom."

Brandon stood, and tucked his pup up under one arm.

Sydney hid a wince as she stood, too. She could only imagine what he may have heard, his office door practically front stage to her and Richard's conversations—or more accurately defined as confrontations. She could only guess what he might think of her. Only a handful of staff had embraced the hybrid classes. Big changes happened slowly in small towns.

"Anyway, thanks again. I really do appreciate your help. Bailey here is still too young to behave himself. When his collar broke, I thought he was a goner for sure if I couldn't catch him before he decided to chase a squirrel into the woods or something. You were a Godsend." Brandon reached down and gave Baxter an affectionate scratch behind the ears. "Who's your partner in crime?"

"Oh," she said, glancing back and forth from Brandon to Baxter. "This is Baxter. He loves to run as much as Bailey apparently does. You mentioned a collar breaking. Is your car far from here? I didn't see one on my run around the park."

"Actually, I live a few miles down the highway, so I left it at home. In retrospect, it wasn't as great of an idea since this happened. It's going to be a pain to get him home," Brandon said, still working on keeping Bailey under control. Sydney heard the hopeful undertones in his unvoiced plea.

"Well, I guess I can't just leave you here with him, especially since we work together, and all," Sydney said, only half-jokingly. She was still happy being a recluse, but her conscience wouldn't let her refuse a person so obviously in need. "I live just through those trees," pointing in the direction of the cabin. "I have an extra collar and leash set, and Bailey looks about Baxter's size. Plus you look like you could use a breather. What kind of dog is he?"

"Australian Shepherd. He's a runner, that's for sure. A collar and a breather would be great, thanks!" Brandon readjusted Bailey, holding him like football, as he began following Sydney back to her cabin.

Sydney made a mental assessment of the condition of the house as they walked. No clothes on the floor, grading papers on the table in the nook, and just a couple of dishes in the sink. She tried to remember if she'd left any undies hanging to dry on the shower curtain rod. Even though she was usually a neat freak, it made her stomach sink at the thought of unexpected company. No one but the furniture delivery guys had been in her home—her sanctuary.

"I didn't see any car either," Brandon asked, intrigued.

Baxter bounced all around them dying to play with Bailey again. Sydney had to work to keep him from wrapping them both up in his leash.

"Like I said, I live just through those trees." Sydney cut across the rest of the access road and headed for the trees, trying not to smile at the confused look on Brandon's face.

"You're kidding, right? How'd you get so lucky having your own personal park entrance?"

"Actually, I found it completely by accident," she explained, as she ducked under the tree branches that hid the path home. On the other side, she pulled the branches back for Brandon. Bailey seemed to realize they were going home with Baxter, and it was taking both of Brandon's arms to keep his excitement contained.

"When I bought the place I knew it backed up to government land. Later, I found out it was a state park. Even then I had no idea a trail existed. After adopting Baxter, I had a fence built to keep him from getting loose when he came outside to play. When I let him out for the first time alone he discovered the installer had left the gate at the back of the fence open and took off. Luckily, I'd stayed at the door to see his reaction to a new fenced yard so I saw the escape. I ran after him and caught up with him just short of the park access road—his collar had gotten snagged on a tree root he'd been digging under. When I knelt down to release him, I noticed the park road."

"Anyway, I guess the former owner hacked it out. Had it not been for 'Mr. Obedient' here, I'd have never seen it. It's very nicely hidden."

Coming through the last of the brush, she opened the gate for Brandon, barely getting it closed as Bailey managed to wiggle out of his grip and escape again. This time, though, he headed straight for Sydney's back door as if he owned the place.

She could have sworn she heard Brandon growl at the pup. Laughing, Sydney used her keys to unlock the door and let them all inside. Bailey took off exploring the new territory. Baxter chased right along after him.

"You have a hot tub!" Brandon noted enviously, as he entered the door behind her.

"Yes, also a gift from the former owner."

"I've wanted to get one myself. Do you use it often?"

"Sometimes, but not nearly enough. Grading papers and bubbling water don't mix well." Sydney said, smiling.

"Please come in. Would you like some coffee, hot tea, hot chocolate," Sydney offered, as she removed her vest while trying to avoid getting knocked over by the two on the floor. Baxter and Bailey were chasing each other everywhere.

"Any kind of coffee would be great. Black....Bailey, come here!" Brandon tried to catch his dog as he rocketed past, grabbing nothing but air.

"It's all right, let them play. Looks like they're making fast friends," Sydney said, as she headed for the kitchen.

"Need any help?" Brandon offered, as he took off his fleece. The Under Armor beneath left little to the imagination, revealing that running, after Bailey or not, was a regular activity.

"No, but thanks," answered Sydney.

Standing about six foot, his broad shoulders and tastefully sculpted chest were complimented by a narrow waist and firm long legs. The college girls must certainly appreciate staring at him during lectures, she thought to herself. Especially, with his wind-tousled, sandy hair falling just above those whiskey-colored eyes. He had a strong jaw, too, which looked particularly nice with that five o'clock shadow.

Good heavens, what was she thinking? Focus on the coffee, girl! It only stands to reason that an attractive man would be worth noting. It's ok to look at the menu when on a diet right? Did those words just sound false to her own ears? Cheesy, too. Dismissing the discomfiting thoughts, she focused on making the coffee.

Brandon looked around as Sydney made herself busy in the kitchen. Bailey had finished his exploration, and he and Baxter were romping around on the sofa playing tug-of-war with Baxter's sock monkey.

Skeptically eyeing the battleground the dogs had chosen, Brandon called, "is Baxter allowed on the sofa?"

"They're fine, don't worry about it."

Unwilling to sit down in the tug-of-war zone, Brandon spotted the fireplace and decided to make himself useful. Folding the screen and setting it aside, he tossed a few more logs onto the fire. Stirring the lazy embers into dancing flames with the poker, he finished the task to his satisfaction.

Straightening up, he replaced the screen. He looked at the mantle noting no photos of anyone except Baxter and Sydney and a photo of a couple who looked like they'd be old enough to be her parents. The dainty nose and hair coloring of the woman in the picture told him that she was most likely Sydney's mom. The picture of the man revealed where she inherited her beautiful eyes.

While there weren't many personal pictures there were certainly plenty of books. Brandon browsed her library smiling at the broad range of titles. Unlike many people's bookshelves that have a few books stacked artfully between knick-knacks and other ornamentation, Sydney's bookshelf was stuffed floor-to-ceiling with actual books. She had quite a collection, too—leather bound, gilt edged classics from Michele de Montaigne and Edgar Allen Poe to glossy gothic vampire paperback novels and romance books.

Sydney was a bookworm. He could just imagine her in black rimmed glasses, hair twisted up in a bun, dressed in a white dress blouse, pencil skirt, and black heels shushing noisy students in the library. He smiled at that.

Pretending to look at the books, Brandon angled himself to study the photo of Sydney. With her long curly red hair and wide set navy blue eyes, she was stunning. She's the type of woman most men would look for any excuse to talk to.

He especially liked how tall she was, 5'7" maybe, and how she carried herself with confidence. She brought to mind Kate Winslet in Titanic in a way. He wondered if that confidence carried over into all parts of her life besides her fending off Richard's tirades. He sure had enjoyed listening to her intellectually out-maneuver that pompous ass.

The scent of freshly brewed coffee reached him and brought him out of his reverie. Hearing her finishing up in the kitchen Brandon returned his attention to Sydney.

"This place is great," Brandon said, as he scooted the dogs off onto the floor, and dropped down onto the gently worn leather sofa. "Have you lived here long?"

"No, I just moved here the summer before last," Sydney replied, as she walked around the sofa and handed Brandon a mug of hot coffee. Pleased, Brandon noted the "I" and not "we" as he helped himself to one of the biscotti from the plate Sydney sat on the coffee table.

"Thanks for the coffee," Brandon said, carefully taking a sip. "Mmmmm, hazelnut?" he asked.

"Good guess." Sydney sat beside Brandon on the sofa. Bailey and Baxter rebelled at the idea of being relegated to the floor and had taken over the oversized rocking chair next to the fireplace instead— the sock monkey forgotten on the floor.

"I was wondering, am I detecting a bit of an accent? Arkansas... or...Georgia maybe?"

"Texas. You?"

"Seattle."

"Oh, I love that place with its farmers' markets, fresh seafood, and fantastic shopping. Why would you ever move away from there?"

"I wanted a fresh start, and they had an opening at the university. It's not like we're not a few hours' drive from there, so it'll be easy to visit."

"If you don't mind my asking, what brought you from Texas all the way up here? Family?" He hoped he wasn't too obvious as he fished for a little info, but he was curious if the lack of pictures meant no boyfriend somewhere around here. It was strange, as beautiful as she was that she appeared to be alone.

"No. I wanted a break from freelance writing and the conference circuit. I put out feelers for a teaching position, and this was one of the places that made me an offer. I liked the area, all its natural beauty, and just let the wind blow me in this direction. Since my parents' death, and other things, well, let's just say it was time for a change." Sydney dodged exposing too much of her past as she put on her best "I'm-perfectly-happy" smile.

"I can understand a need for change, although I'm sorry to hear about the loss of your parents."

Sydney took a shaky breath, "Thank you. They died several years ago, although it seems like yesterday. It was so sudden. My dad had a heart attack that caught us completely by surprise. To look at him you'd have thought he was the picture of health. My mom took it real hard, too. She missed him terribly and just wasted away. She died within the year. They say that she died of a broken heart. It's still hard to talk about."

"I'm so sorry. They say it's like that with couples who love deeply. They can't stand to be apart."

Sydney's eyes welled up against her will as she tried to hide it behind a forced smile. Great! She thought to herself, this is just not her day. She would not cry!

Brandon pretended not to notice her distress. He wasn't fooled by the smile, but understood the need to move onto easier ground.

"I just moved here myself a few months ago. I love it up here although it's not much different from Seattle. The mountain views are just amazing. I'll bet it's a whole new world for you coming from a place like Texas."

"Yeah, it's pretty amazing."

Sensing she'd regained a modicum of control, he asked, "How are you finding life at the university?"

"Well, it's good to be back in an institutional setting," Sydney stopped short at her odd choice of words, and then laughed at his bemused expression. "That's not quite how I meant it to sound, but, sometimes it does get a little crazy."

"I'd bet. I'm sure Richard isn't making it any easier."

Sydney blushed as she rolled her eyes in mock exasperation to the reference of Richard. She realized with a certainty that the heated debates between her and Richard had indeed spilled over into Brandon's office.

"He's not exactly taking the hint that I just don't agree with him on a few of his policies."

"Richard does that to everyone from what I've heard, and get to hear, for that matter. I get front-row-center to his outbursts, since my office is right across the hall from his classroom."

"Lovely," Sydney said, not feeling the least bit better knowing she wasn't Richard's only victim. Misery doesn't necessarily love company, and she felt sorry for anyone who crossed swords with him.

"You're the first, I hear, that's really stood up to him," continued Brandon, "I get the feeling it threatens him on some level he doesn't like."

"Mind if I help myself," Brandon gestured toward the kitchen with his mug.

"No, go ahead."

Brandon got up and refreshed his coffee. "Since I started working here, I notice most people, when they become the focus of Richard's unwanted attention, just smile, say I see your point, and let it rest. Sometimes it works, but then Richard thinks he's won."

Sitting back down, he continued, "I must say, it's been fun listening to you take him on. I'm glad you persuaded the school board to allow hybrid classes. Even though they're the norm at the larger universities, this is a small university in a rural area, and getting that kind of change had to have been tough."

Sydney tried to ignore how the admiration in his voice made her feel. With Richard being such a problem, and not quite having the full endorsement from the board, it was a welcome change to hear praise about the changes she was making.

"I guess it's something that I feel passionate about. People, especially parents, single parents, working adults, all deserve to be able to get an education and earn a grade unhindered by being chained to a desk because their grades depend on it. Richard does that," said Sydney. "Students can't miss more than three classes, sans a life or death emergency, before their grade falls one letter grade per absence thereafter. That's ridiculous. Especially, since he's applying the same rule to a single kid that usually has no children and gets financial support from their family, to our non-traditional students who have more responsibility— like a parent."

"A lot of these non-traditional student-parents have an established career, more often than not. Sometimes that job must take priority over school, and the student might have to work late and miss a class. Richard's rules make those choices harder because he penalizes their grades for absences he doesn't deem worthy. He should remember that a student's income is not only supporting his own paycheck, but also their kids' meals, doctors' bills, mortgage payments, and everything else. It is our responsibility as faculty and staff to help them achieve their education. Not stand in the way of it, and penalizing them on their GPA is persecutory."

"Eventually, Richard will have to adapt. Many colleges have already gone to hosting complete online degree programs in many states—no in-person class time required. So what if we haven't officially adopted entire online degree programs, and all of our classes are still on campus? We can still offer some flexibility to our students."

Sydney noted Brandon's bemused expression. "I'm sorry, I didn't mean to go on and on, it's just I wish Richard would let it go."

"No, I completely understand, and I agree with you. Richard's making your life difficult. He seems to be something of a control freak. I think he fears his way of teaching, the only life he's ever known to be fair, is coming to an end. What he has excelled at is becoming obsolete. Your ideas and changes are threatening his existence."

"Great. I hate dealing with control freaks, and I'm sorry, but it's hard to feel sorry for him when he's being such a jerk."

"Ha, sorry. Just hang in there. The board is seeing the progress you're making, and eventually, the situation will take care of itself."

"Thanks. I hope so. So, school counselor, huh? Does that keep you very busy? I mean, I wouldn't think there would be many kids who seek out counseling at this age. Or am I wrong?" Sydney said, as she fished around for something to end the awkward subject of her ongoing feud with Richard.

"Well," Brandon thought carefully, "I recently just started taking clients again, so it's not keeping me too busy. I focused on just teaching for a while."

That hedging sounded a little familiar. Sydney wondered if there was a story behind that statement, but didn't voice her question. She didn't want anyone poking around in her past, either.

"Do you get many interesting cases?"

"There are always the typical ones." Sighing, he continued. "I have a disheartening one right now that really gets to me. I'm currently working with a young lady who goes to school here, and her husband is abusing her. It's been going on a while. He doesn't understand her desire to get an education. It's not just that, he tries to control her entire life, too. She still loves him, though, so she's torn on whether or not to leave him. His actions are all over the place— from making wild promises to do better if she'll only stay, to saying things like if he can't have her then no one can. She's questioning her decision to leave him, and wanting to know if it's possible if his promises to change could be on the up and up, or if he could really make good on those threats of his."

"I've told her that only he knows if he's willing to work for a change, but no conversion is immediate. Only time will tell, is all I can tell her. That if he's truly willing to change it will take time, and he'll make mistakes along the way. I can't make the decision for her, and I think that's what she's wanting. I warned her though that she should take no chances with her safety."

"Oh, I can't understand it! Why is it that a man tries to control a woman instead of loving her, and why is he surprised the relationship suffers and dies, and that she eventually decides she's better off without him? I can't believe he threatened her!"

"Yeah, I know. I wish I could do more to help her. I wish I could read her mind sometimes. Plus, if he really wants the relationship to work, it would help if he came to counseling, too," said Brandon. "It's hard to tell if this relationship is salvageable if you only hear one side, and only one person's working toward saving it."

Sydney went on. "I was married to someone like that. My ex was controlling and verbally abusive. He had quite a temper, too. I'd find myself constantly analyzing what I did to set him off, second-guessing myself, and wondering if something was going on at work or something else. All the while, I was constantly looking for ways to please him."

"Finally, things would come to a head, and I'd explode right back. I'd get fed up with trying to make him happy, and having my efforts thrown back in my face. I'd lose my temper, and there would be a big fight. I'd ask him if he wanted me to leave, because clearly I wasn't making him happy. Eventually, he'd apologize, and be on his best behavior for a short while. For a while, I'd think that it was going to be OK. It wasn't long, maybe a few months at best, that things would be good, but then the abuse would gradually start all over again. Eventually, I had to face the sad truth that I'd married an abuser who really wasn't sorry enough to change. I definitely feel for the girl."

"That's what I'm afraid is happening to her. She seems to want to take the majority of the blame onto herself. She almost acts as if she is apologizing to me when she's describing how he's treating her. As if she's accepted she's to blame, but a little part of her hopes she's not, and she's just not sure," sighed Brandon.

"I can relate to that, too. For a long time I thought it was me, and that somehow I kept making him mad, or I wasn't good enough for him, and that I deserved it somehow. I was painfully aware I wasn't perfect, and it was easier to blame myself."

"Does she have family?"

Brandon shook his head no. "She's not close with her parents, and she doesn't seem to have any close friends, either. So for all intents and purposes, she's alone."

"It's hard to be without family. I married right after my parents died. I really didn't have anyone to talk to about problems in my marriage. Even people at church weren't that helpful. Divorce is not an option in many faiths."

"My ex didn't like me having friends, either. I read somewhere years later that people like that try to isolate their victims. I'm surprised he let me go to college. I suppose that he knew he didn't have a leg to stand on since I used the money given to me by my parents in their will. I wanted to be a teacher, to teach English, and I was interested in Journalism, too. Writing had always come naturally for me."

"One day, after a particularly bad fight, I was extremely depressed. I felt if I didn't get it out of my system I would explode. I started writing out how I felt, and just dumping the whole sordid mess onto paper. It was therapeutic—cathartic. An added benefit was I rediscovered how much I loved to write. I got involved with a local writers group, wrote an article here and there for the newspaper, and that led to freelance writing. I decided to write for a living instead of teach, so I focused my efforts in that direction."

"I finally broke away from my ex completely when my freelance writing started to take off, and other people's observations of me began to reshape my view of who I really was. Where he saw a loser, they saw a bright and talented woman who could do just about anything she set her mind to. It was almost like meeting the real me for the first time."

"I hope something like that will happen for your patient. Once I started seeing myself truthfully, I began to read up on abusers and realized he was a really insecure person. No matter how hard you try, it'll never be good enough because it's not you they're unhappy with, it's themselves. Hopefully, she'll gradually start to see herself truthfully through her own eyes, and see there's a better life out there, even though it can be scary starting over. A part of my way of dealing with the divorce, and working through all that baggage, was writing it all down."

"I'll mention writing to her and see if she enjoys that or has any other hobbies that could be an outlet, but, for now, I've referred her to a support group for battered wives since she has no family to help her along. He was only physically abusive once, but psychologically she has all the symptoms of battered-wives syndrome."

Brandon stopped at the sadness on her face, and the concern she obviously felt over a nameless girl. "I'm sorry, Sydney, this must be dredging up a lot of memories for you. Right after you lost your parents, to go into a bad marriage? Wow, I'm really sorry to hear that."

The sorrow in his eyes was too much to take. She didn't need or want his pity. Her ex was an idiot. She was over that drama. She'd come to terms with him not loving her. David's betrayal—not so much.

Sydney stood, and walked back to the kitchen to fix more coffee.

"It's ok. I'm fine now, and I don't mind talking about it if it helps someone else find the courage to escape. I'm making some more coffee....interested?"

"Yes, please."

Sydney grabbed some fruit and cheese to prepare, as well.

"So how about you?" she said, as she busied herself in the kitchen.

"I see no ring. Have you ever been married or are you a confirmed bachelor?" attempting a joke at his expense.

Brandon winced. "Well, I was married, too."

"Oh, I'm sorry. You don't have to..." Sydney began, already sorry she'd asked.

"No, it's ok. Fair's, fair," he said with a laugh. "She was my high school sweetheart—my first love. Nothing so cliché as the football team captain and the head cheerleader, but we dated all through high school. It was always expected that we'd be married someday, and we did. Just after graduation. We even attended college and graduated together. No kids though, she didn't want any. Turns out, she didn't want me very much either. I came home early from the office one day due to a sick headache, and found my wife and my best friend together."

Sydney's hand flew to cover her gaping mouth!

Seeing her reaction Brandon added with a rueful grin, "It's ok, they weren't actually in the *middle* of anything. They were already done, though not yet *fully* dressed. However, with the evidence it was plain enough to see what had been going on."

"Anyway, I exploded as best I could with a migraine pounding in my head, as my best friend from college made a real quick exit. She and I fought, of course. I mean, how could she, right? Within hours she was packing, too. Apparently, the affair had started freshman year of college. It had been going on under my nose the entire time. In one afternoon, I'd lost everything—my wife *and* my best friend."

"She tried to apologize. She said she loved us both, and she said thought she loved me more, but, as the affair continued, she found out she was wrong. She wanted him. She swore was going to tell me, but hadn't found the right time."

"Ha! Like there's a right time! It's kind of funny now."

"Anyway, I was pretty shaken up back then. For years I'd thought I was in this wonderful relationship with my wife, and best friends with one of the greatest guys you could ever hope to be friends with, only to find out it had all been a lie. I was the last to know."

"Within days I realized I had lost the will to practice psychology, too, so I lost my practice as well. I had no choice but to temporarily abandon trying to build my clientele. My emotional state was just too unbalanced, and I sure didn't feel like I was in the right frame of mind to counsel others at that time. A colleague took on the few clients I had, and I quit."

"I went back to college for my teaching certificate, got a job at a university, and then buried myself in my work. Teaching took my mind off the past, left little time to try again with women, kept me busy almost one hundred percent of the time, and gave me the time I needed to get over everything. So I literally 'worked' my way through it." He laughed at that.

"I can relate," Sydney said, carrying the coffee back to the living room, and sat a tray of sliced fruit, diced cheeses, slivers of summer sausage and crackers on the table before sitting back down.

"Looks great. I'm starved!"

Sydney smiled at his enthusiasm.

"Anyway, I just recently decided it was time to begin taking patients again. They already had a therapist where I worked, so I looked around for a position with a counseling gig on the side, and here I am!"

"They, however," continued Brandon as he filled his plate, "went right on as if it was perfectly natural to destroy a marriage. She acted as if we'd never been together and moved literally from our home into his. Can you believe it?"

Sydney shook her head in astonishment.

"My friend tried to patch things up, I think more out of guilt than anything else, but I couldn't stand the sight of him. She never looked back. They were married within days of our divorce being final, and live 'happily ever after'—or so I've heard. She even decided she *did* want kids. She now has a toddler and another one on the way."

"For years it was pure hell. In some ways, I wondered if it would be easier if she were dead, than happily prancing around with my best friend."

Sydney, who'd been leaning in to grab her coffee cup, froze instantly. Pain sliced through her heart. Tears welled up in her eyes. She couldn't breathe for a moment. The memories came back with brutal force, and bringing with it a tidal wave of emotion raging into her heart.

"Never, ever, say that."

The vicious calm in her voice shocked Brandon.

"Sydney, I didn't mean...it's just an expression." Brandon couldn't fathom the raw emotion in her voice or why the color had suddenly drained from her face.

"Never wish someone is dead. Never. Death is permanent. There is no redemption for wrongs done, no second chances, no possibility for future happiness or to make up for lost time, no possibilities for anything...nothing. When someone dies there is no chance to set anything right, to forgive, to be forgiven, to say I love you, to make a difference." Raw emotion choked Sydney into silence. Damn it all she was going to lose it in front of not only a new acquaintance, but a colleague as well.

Blindly Sydney turned her back to Brandon, and headed for the bedroom door as she mumbled, "excuse me." Before she could escape, though, two strong warm arms gently, but firmly, engulfed her from behind. Sidling over to the sofa Sydney had fled from, Brandon brought her back down to sit, still holding her to him. He allowed her to pour out her torment in the shelter and comfort of his arms, while permitting her to keep a modicum of dignity by letting her face away from him while she wept. Burying her head into the crook of his shoulder Sydney sobbed as her body wracked and shuddered with each breath.

She couldn't stop the flood gates. They were open, and the torrent unleashed. Her parents were dead, David was gone—oh God, she couldn't bring any of them back. Embarrassment washed through her at her lack of control.

Brandon cursed himself for a fool. Hadn't she just mentioned her parent's death still feeling like it was yesterday? It's obvious her loss was still fresh.

Handing Sydney the napkin off her plate he continued to hold her as he silently wished he could take the words back, but knowing her crying it out would speed some healing her way.

When her grief was spent, and she was down to random sighs and sniffs, he realized it was time to let her go. He was a little surprised to find that he didn't want to. She had felt very right in his arms.

❧ He loosened his hold and waited quietly until she was ready to talk. Giving Sydney some breathing room, Brandon stood, gathered up the already used napkin, and took it to the kitchen to the trash. He grabbed her a fresh one on his way back.

Sydney accepted it, and smiled her thanks.

"Looks like you've needed to do that for a while, huh?" Brandon half-heartedly joked.

"Yeah, I hate being a girl and being all weepy," Sydney countered back.

Brandon chuckled at her feigned attempt at orneriness, as he nonchalantly sat back down beside her. He picked up his plate, and casually started eating as if nothing had happened, giving her more time.

Sydney wiped off her face with her napkin. Removing her hair from the scrunchie, she combed through it with her fingers in an attempt to make herself a little more presentable.

Turning in her seat to face him Sydney drew her knees up to her chest and hugged them with her arms, ready to face the music. Sort of.

"I'm sorry. This has been a really emotional day for me, and I didn't mean to unload on you. God, how did we get this far so fast? I just met you! I'm sorry I snapped just then. It's just so unfair when someone dies unexpectedly. I didn't even get to say good-bye. I'm tired of losing the people I love."

"I know, I know. You don't have to apologize to me. It's no big deal. I'm sorry, though. I shouldn't have said it that way either," Brandon reassured her.

"I know you didn't mean anything by it—it just caught me off guard. I guess I just needed a good cry—cleans out the radiator so the car can run right, so to speak. Know what I mean?" She smiled at her own metaphorical joke. "I'm fine, really. If you don't mind, though, I'd rather not talk about it anymore. OK?"

Sydney stared into the fire and hoped he'd leave it be. Her self-consciousness was riding her hard. She was ready to be done.

"I understand. Hey, I know just the thing. For rescuing me from a night of searching for an ungrateful runaway dog, the loan of the collar and leash, and the snack, how about letting me take you for a quick bite at the local tavern?"

"I really appreciate the offer, and the shoulder," Sydney smiled sheepishly, "but how about I give you a ride home and take a rain check? I've got a lot of papers to grade still, and I'm pretty exhausted from all the excitement. OK?"

Getting up Sydney took the tray and mugs back to the kitchen, and put some distance between them— adding a little emphasis to her words.

Brandon took his cue and got up, too. He grabbed his fleece, and then put the loaned leash and collar on a gently snoring Bailey.

"Fair enough," he replied, "but I'm holding you to it! You have no clue what a devil it is to find this little beggar when he gets loose. I owe you big."

Sydney laughed, knowing full well what it was like to try to find Baxter when he'd gotten out. She put on her coat and grabbed her purse. Baxter woke to the sound of jangling keys and ran to Sydney, begging for a ride.

"Oh, but I do," Sydney laughed as she lovingly scratched Baxter's ears. "I do."

Snapping a leash on Baxter, Sydney led them out of the house.

Sydney followed Brandon's directions and arrived at his home. He lived a few miles away, just as he'd said. Unlike her location on the border of the park, his home was across the road. Instead of being surrounded by forest, his land was lightly treed, and overlooked a farming valley.

"Oh, it's lovely," Sydney exclaimed, upon seeing the stone house. While her house was made entirely of cedar, Brandon's was made completely of Hiawatha stone. The house reminded her of an English stone cottage—solid and formidable.

It was square with uniform double windows on either side of the doorway and three windows across the top floor. Each window had a pair of gray shutters which appeared functional rather than decorative. The wood door had black metal hinges and was painted a dark gray. It had a tiny window at the top. The tiny window had its own little door and a little metal grill, too. Very medieval, she thought to herself.

Rising up on the right side of the cottage was a fireplace chimney. The roof appeared to be something like slate from what she could see peering out from under the snow. Hardy English Ivy crawled its way across the face of the house adding a splash of snow tipped green to the monochromatic scene.

He had a detached garage, too, made of the same sturdy stone, and a matching slate-like roof. The wooden doors were made to mimic the front door, sans the little window. She wondered idly if there had been some sort of home owners association at one time that required detached garages.

Unlike her home, his faced away from the main road maximizing the available view of the picturesque valley.

"Thanks," said Brandon. "I thought my house was pretty special until I saw yours. Would you like to see inside?"

"I'll take a rain check on that, too, but thank you. It's been a long day."

"Alright. See you at school." Brandon and Bailey hopped out of the car.

Brandon waved at her when he paused to unlock his door. Sydney waved back, backed her car out of the drive, and headed home.

~ Attendance over the next few weeks had dwindled down into what she affectionately referred to as "the regulars." These would be the students she would see in person for most of the remainder of the semester. During class discussions Sydney would place more names with faces. A few had yet to show. Although rare, it had happened before that a student or two never showed up for one of her classes, but she'd usually met them in her office or elsewhere on campus. Having a student not show up had never really bothered her before. This time she felt an unsettling sensation as she noted Emily hadn't shown up, yet.

Brandon, however, did. He kept the conversations to small talk and school subjects and thankfully didn't bring up the day in her cabin. He certainly made it clear he was her friend. Problem was, it seemed he might be interested in being more than friends. She wasn't sure she was anywhere near ready for that, although she'd certainly opened up to him in a way unlike any other.

She still didn't know what had happened that day. It wasn't in her nature to open up to a stranger like that. It'd been a long time since she'd sat and visited with anyone, for that matter. It was all too weird, and it was disconcerting how often her mind drifted to his strong arms and solid chest. It was all she could do to forget how it felt as he held her. Even in her grief her mind registered the solid warmth. Even now her whole body craved to feel him hold her like that again, and that was dangerous.

He'd asked again about dinner, and if she had plans on Valentine's Day. She said she'd think about it, not wanting to abruptly turn him down. While she wasn't ready for a relationship, she did like the idea of having a friend. At the same time, she felt a need to keep him at arm's length.

She realized that Brandon had mistaken her grief solely due to her parents' death and that he knew nothing about David. Sooner or later, if he was interested in more than just friendship, she would have to explain how she felt. How she couldn't trust anyone right now. How deeply she'd been betrayed. How broken she still felt. She wasn't ready for that either.

In the end, she declined the invitation using the excuse that she'd have way too many papers being turned in that Friday and knew she'd be busy all weekend. Plus, she wasn't sure what to expect from Emily, and would rather be alone if her paper triggered another emotional avalanche. He took it well. He smiled as he voiced his understanding and finagled a rain check from her in return. Again.

⁂ The second essays arrived on Friday. The assignment was to write an Argumentative essay and pick a topic to defend. Sydney searched immediately for Emily's paper. She'd yet to see Emily in class. After the initial shock of reading her first essay Sydney wanted to meet this girl.

Argumentative
Creative Writing
Emily Halliwell

All Need Unconditional Love

I do not understand how I can be who I am, so wonderful of a person, and no one wants to value me enough to keep me— to fight for us? Why are people afraid of giving themselves wholly to another person and finding the completion of oneself in the giving? Of the fullness of beginning where another ends and finding your end is in their beginning? What is so wrong with that? What is so scary about being loved for everything about who and what you are without judgment and without reservation? Why is it so hard to be open and truthful instead of living in lies and worrying about getting caught?

Lies and half-truths are restraints and a weight that buries a person in a world of darkness and self-loathing. Their lives are caught up in a cover-up. They are not fully open to living because they are always looking over their shoulder trying not to let the world see who they really are. They are caught in a world of confusion and rationalization. Torn between the truth and lies and sometimes not knowing or caring which is the truth and which is the lie— taking what feels good, regardless, to fill the void they have created in the lie. Running from themselves, and hoping not to get caught with the evidence. I remember being that person and living that life. I have the scars.

Openness is a freedom. And it is exposing and difficult if you do not love yourself and feel you must hide yourself. But when you do begin to be free to love yourself unconditionally you are free indeed.

Unconditional love is the most freeing love in the world. It allows the giver to fully accept oneself and another, and in doing so releases the boundaries of all the petty things that eventually wear a relationship down from its initial joy to the acceptable level of only liking just a part of them instead of cherishing all of them—the good and the bad.

The receiver, to them, it is coming home. It is finding your home in the heart of another— it is peace and rest, it is comfort and solace. It is knowing you belong— you are an integral part of another and you are not alone. Not to say there is never a conflict, but even the conflict is held in a light that doesn't have the aire of danger, but rather of life happening— and knowing that it is not a threat to the relationship, but a growth to it.

These two parts, the giver and the receiver, are reciprocal. Both benefit and it becomes a synchronicity—a symbiosis—what I fully think God had in mind with us and in our relationships, and in marriage. You are still yourself, you still have your space and you are your own person, but you are no longer fragmented. You are whole.

I know I am not in any way the perfect person, but I feel I have so much love to give in the purest form of the emotion. It seems to be the thing I need most and cannot live without. It is a need I feel more strongly than any other. I can be happy in any home, any state, any job, any situation, yet I cannot live without love.

Openness and honesty. Lies and cover-ups. Sydney wondered which she really had with David. It was clear he'd been covering things up or he wouldn't have left the way he did—abandoning her without hope of reconciliation. No second chances. Nothing.

What if he had loved her like Emily described? What if he loved himself that much? Would he then have been able to love her fully in return? Would it have made a difference? Would he still be there? Things happen for a reason, don't they? Sydney didn't know.

Turning to the next paper, she ignored the thoughts swirling in her head. She wasn't running from the ghosts of her past tonight, and she wasn't entertaining them either. She had to focus on the here and now.

❦ Valentine's Day had sucked. There were plenty of papers, but not enough to keep her as busy has she had led Brandon to believe. She wondered if he'd had a boring weekend, too. She hoped not. Especially, since she had said she couldn't go out. Should she have accepted his invitation? No. She wasn't ready, yet.

What if another relationship fails like her ex? Or she falls in love and loses them like she did her parents? Or God forbid like David? Sure she was doing all right now, coping with all that had happened in the last few years, but could she survive another loss? Was she willing to find out? She didn't know. Instead of jogging, she spent the day shoveling a path in the snow from her door to the garage. She'd be busy with work tomorrow.

Sydney left for work early the next day. The snow began to taper off, and was becoming less and less heavy as the temperature edged closer to the double digits. The landscape was still covered in white, making it easy to catch a glimpse of the redbirds, and a lone coyote, as she drove past. Pretty soon they'd blend back into the scenery when the world returned to the colors of spring and shed its winter coat.

It's funny how the redbird never changes color. Rather it loses its place of prominence in the landscape when the world colorfully springs to life again from the gray grip of winter. She knew that the pain of David's loss would be like that, one day—still a painful splash of memory, but one that would lessen as she learned to live in a world of color again.

Sydney entered the building and noted Brandon was already in his office. Slipping past his door she made her way to her own closet. Grabbing her mail from the box she found a plain colored manila envelope with her first name on it. Opening it, she had to laugh. Brandon had left her a little box of candy hearts. Oh no, she thought. Those things were awful! She couldn't decide on whether to eat one or just draw on the sidewalk with it.

She should go thank him, maybe ask how his weekend was. Before she had finished the thought he stuck his head in the door.

"Good morning, Sydney."

"Brandon, good morning," Sydney smiled in welcome. "Thank you for the candy, you *really* shouldn't have."

"I know, but I wanted to. I saw them on the shelf at the campus bookstore and thought it'd be funny. If you're not busy again, we can take Bailey and Baxter out for a run after work, and you can work off all the calories. I know they'd love to see each other again. Bailey cries at the door like he's lost his best friend."

Sydney laughed at the thought. Going for the sympathy vote, was he?

"Sounds good to me. Baxter has been moping a little, too. Oh, and you're welcome to park in my driveway and we'll start from there."

"Perfect. See ya around 6."

Over the next two weeks Brandon became a consistent jogging buddy, arriving at 6 with Bailey, and jogging the park with her and Baxter. Sydney found the routine comfortable and looked forward to the visits. It was nice having a friend again.

Brandon still sensed that Sydney needed space, only stayed for a light round of small talk, and then promptly excused himself to his own grading. He was careful to not impose and never pushed for an invitation to stay.

Sydney smiled as she realized his thoughtfulness. She still wasn't sure what to think about Brandon. Sitting down to her pile of papers to grade, she found she didn't have much time to think anyway.

This week's essay focused on comparison and contrast. As she dug for the envelope that she'd come to recognize as coming from Emily, Sydney again noted that she continued to be conspicuously absent from class. Even the kids that took the most liberty with her attendance policy showed up at least once or twice at her office. Or emailed.

Maybe she had a good reason. Maybe she's the mother of a small child and couldn't come to class. Maybe one of her essays would give up some clues. Sydney pulled out the essay and began to read.

Comparison and Contrast
Creative Writing
Emily Halliwell

The Other Sides of Me

Friendship is something that too many people take for granted. Moreover, it is not nearly valued enough as the true gift that it is. I am lucky enough to have had two close friends in my life. They were kindred spirits of mine.

The first and closest, he and I were most alike. We were like two souls who have known one another throughout the passage of time— quietly recognizing each other once they meet again. He was a sanctuary, a place where there was openness and honesty, a place of just "being" with no designs or assignations. I saw myself in his eyes. We were the same. And the joy of being understood was unsurpassed.

We laughed when the other was happy and our tears were shed for the others pain. We spoke of everything and of nothing. There was no judgment even when deserved. My most intimate thoughts I could reveal, and he completed the thought oftentimes as if it were his own. He touched me in a way that few have ever done— he provided the affectionate edification of the soul. He was a place of peace.

So intrinsic was the connection that I was my most careful with this friendship. I was my most accommodating for him, and even when we were apart, I took respite in just knowing he was there. In a world that is as cold and as bitter as the depths of winter, he was like returning to the revitalizing warmth of a cherry fire. Rare is it in life to meet someone who feels like home. With this friend, our lives touched where the heart, mind and soul touch.

However, my other friend was special in a different way. We were not as alike as the first, but we had enough. We were both alone. So we would seek each other out now and then, to pretend—to share one brief moment holding one another. We provided for each other the touch, the caress, and the comfort of another's care, allowing ourselves to remember how it felt to be physically loved.

His arm would cradle my head. I kissed his hand. The warmth of his breath fell on my shoulder. The soft-spoken words mirrored the hand that caressed my face as sweetly as his words fell upon my ears. I'd lie spent in the arms of one who cares. Knowing it was not love, we'd pretend together. We'd pretend for a moment we are not alone, we were not hurting. And when we became too weary-worn by the world we would come together, to share our pain— to gain the courage once again to face the world on our own—alone.

He and I only touched on the physical level. We cared, and on some levels besides the physical we could relate—but not to the depths and breadth of the other friend. And we understand that what we had is temporal and there was nothing but a borrowed solace to be found. Our days together were numbered. His passage from my life was sad, but it was to be expected. For this second friendship was built on a different foundation than the first. However, it was beautiful nonetheless.

Both were the closest friends I have had and I miss them deeply. Their absence is a painful hollow in my soul. In our individual relationships, we provided for the other the completion that we all need—love, intimacy, understanding, and home. They are my inspiration that someday I may find both relationships in one—that I will find the other side of me.

Sydney felt the quiet tears roll down her face. What a fool she'd been to think that she'd never love again. Yes, she'd had a hateful ex, and, yes, there'd been David who'd cruelly abandoned her, but never loving again was a foolish vow. At the time she had made the decision to swear off relationships, it had seemed right—but it wasn't. Emily was right. One day, some day, she knew she'd want to find that "home." So far she wasn't ready. She recognized, however, that she was going to be ready someday.

"*Our days together are numbered.*" That line haunted Sydney. What if she'd missed out on meeting the right person, and her opportunity had passed her by already? Sydney didn't know, but she would try to start opening herself up for the opportunity to find love again. If Brandon was the one, she didn't want to make the mistake of losing out on what could be the other side of herself. Saving her papers for the rest of the weekend, Sydney readied herself for bed—her last thoughts were full.

~ Saturday morning dawned with a list of errands to run. She spent the day in town checking one thing after another off of her to-do list. Coming home with a car packed with groceries, a treat for Baxter, and a pizza as her Saturday night indulgence, her favorite radio weather man announced an incoming blast of snow was expected later that evening. Some area accumulation could be up to a foot or more with blizzard-like conditions possible. It had begun snowing before she left and had already shown several inches of accumulation by the time she arrived home. Hearing that, Sydney was glad she couldn't decide what kind of pizza she wanted and had splurged on an extra-large—half Canadian bacon and pineapple and half green pepper and onion. YUM! It sounded like she'd be staying home the rest of the weekend. Whatever side of the pizza she didn't have tonight, would make a great breakfast or lunch tomorrow!

After eating, Sydney began grading papers again. Baxter brought his newly acquired raw hide chew up onto the chair with her and was soon fast asleep, his treat carefully tucked under his chin.

Hours passed as the stack of papers dwindled down. Sydney yawned and got up to get a drink. Baxter rose with her, but instead of going to the back door to be let out, he ran to the front door, barking madly. Casting him an inquisitive look, Sydney continued toward the kitchen until the knocking began. Who the heck could be out on a night like this, she wondered? Sydney headed for the door. Opening it, she found the blizzard in full force and Brandon holding Bailey. Both were soaked to the skin.

"Oh, my God, what happened?" Sydney gasped, ushering Brandon inside toward the fire. Bailey yipped in response to Baxter's welcoming bark, but remained uncharacteristically subdued in Brandon's arms as Brandon positioned Bailey and himself on the hearth, as close to the fire as he could get.

Sydney rushed for blankets and towels as Brandon explained what happened through chattering teeth.

"Bailey got out again. With the onset of the storm I had to go and look for him. Luckily, I caught him about a mile from here on the main road, but on our way home, a dog or a fox or something bounded in front of the car. I swerved, and now it's stuck in the snow about a half mile from here. I hope you don't mind, but I couldn't make it home in this weather— not walking."

"No, of course, not. Don't be silly," Sydney said hastily, as she made a beeline for the kitchen after giving Brandon the blanket and towels. "I'll start some hot coffee, and you get out of those wet clothes. Wrap yourself up in the blanket. I don't have anything for you to wear, but you can't stay like that. The bedroom's behind you. Please, help yourself."

Bailey, still wrapped in his towel, stayed behind on the hearth, as Brandon obeyed.

"How are the roads?" Sydney called.

"Not good. They're wet from the previous snowmelt, and the temp is below freezing, so it's very slick. The worst of it is the wind, though. It's a near white-out."

Sydney looked outside. Discovering she was unable to see the tree line, she immediately decided Brandon was right. Now that he and Bailey were safe, there was no good reason to try to help him home. He and Baxter's buddy were staying the night. Sydney felt a little ill. Spending the night?! In her home?

"So how did he get out?"

"I was balancing my briefcase, laptop and cell phone while looking through the mail as I walked in the front door, and it all fell. Struggling to catch the laptop distracted me from the door. The wind grabbed it, flung it open, and he took off. I was in so much of a hurry to keep him in sight I didn't even stop to get the leash."

Brandon emerged from her room wrapped in the blanket toga-style with the bath towel draped across his shoulders. Sydney met him at the sofa to take his wet dress clothes from him, then headed toward the laundry room.

"He headed toward your place, and I thought I was saved there for a moment. Then he ran right on by chasing something I couldn't see. I think the snow got to him after about a mile past here, though, because he stopped as if he was waiting for me, then came running when I pulled over, thank God."

"Anyway, I called for a tow truck from the car, and they won't be able to come pull me out until tomorrow. There doesn't seem to be too much damage, but I'll take it into the shop in the morning just to be safe."

"Sydney, I tried to call." Brandon said. "I'm so sorry to barge in on you like this..."

"Oh, don't worry about it. I tend to forget to turn my cell phone on after class, so I didn't hear it." Sydney called from the laundry room, pouring every ounce of reassurance into her voice.

She hugged herself and prayed for strength. What was she scared of? Taking a deep breath, she called herself a coward, started the dryer and forced herself to emerge from her temporary hiding place. "I'm just glad I live so close, you know?" Which *was* a good thing, she reminded herself. "You couldn't make it another five miles to your place walking in this storm, and, had you stayed in your car, you would have been stuck with Bailey trying to stay warm all night."

She sounded calm, right?

"Even if you could manage to spend the night in the car out in that mess, how could you let him go out to use the bathroom without a leash?" Speaking more to reassure herself than him, "He doesn't seem to have the common sense God gave a flea, though!"

Spying Brandon's ruined dress shoes, she found the resolution she needed to back her decision.

"And I'm surprised you made it this far in your dress shoes and trench coat. Not an ounce of tread on those I'd wager. It's a wonder you didn't slip, fall and break your neck. I mean really, Brandon, you weren't dressed at all for this weather."

Brandon chuckled at her scolding as he carefully laid the contents of his wallet out to dry on the counter.

"So, you're stuck here, and we'll make the best of it. Have you eaten?"

Brandon smiled, and shook his head, no. He was relieved she was going to be OK with this. He knew she was definitely hesitant about their burgeoning friendship and would be uncomfortable with this situation. He loved her all the more that she was able to master her fear so quickly. Love? Whoa. Where did that come from?

"Good, I have pizza. Do you like green peppers and onions?"

"Sounds great. I'm so hungry I could eat the box, too!"

Sydney laughed at that. "Come on, Caesar," poking fun at the toga getup he had fashioned out of the blanket, "let's get you some pizza."

He headed for the kitchen after glancing back at a soundly sleeping Bailey—Baxter laying guard at his feet.

Brandon ate while good-naturedly enduring more lectures on not having an emergency kit in his car that included a blanket, water, snacks, as well as, not keeping a spare leash and a change of clothes in there, too. She will make a great mom someday, he thought.

Sydney left him to his thoughts after dinner while she showered and changed into some sweats and fuzzy socks. Still coming to terms with having an overnight guest, she began to dry her hair as she racked her brains for what to do. She couldn't just ignore him and curl up with a book, but she wasn't much of the entertainer, either.

She wasn't sure why she was nervous. He wasn't the kind of guy who'd try anything. In fact, he'd been nothing but a perfect gentleman. Still. She shook her head. Nope, no "still." Everything will be fine. The sofa was big enough for him to sleep on. She was safe, and things would go back to normal tomorrow. It was fine. She had tons of movies. That's it! That'd make it less awkward.

Brandon's pants and dress shirt were dry by the time she finished drying her hair. While he changed back into his clothes she stoked the fire. Her shower had done little to lessen the knots in her shoulders, but she felt better now that she had a plan to entertain her unexpected guest. Sydney grabbed some popcorn and started it in the microwave. She'd just find a nice explosive action adventure film and they could settle in and watch TV until bedtime. She had started to smile to herself, satisfied with her plan just as the microwave dinged. And, as if on cue, the power went out.

"You have got to be kidding me! Really!?"

"Got a circuit breaker I could check?" Brandon asked.

"Already on it," Sydney called, as she headed for the laundry room. A few seconds later she emerged with a box of candles. "It's not that. Must be the storm."

Suddenly, the room seemed way too small and the fire way too intimate as Sydney scattered and lit a dozen candles. What the heck were they supposed to do now?

"Is that popcorn I smell?"

"Yeah, to go with the movie, I thought we'd watch. Want some?"

"Sure, I can get it. Where are the bowls?"

"Under the center island on the end nearest the laundry room," replied Sydney, as she finished setting out and lighting candles in the bedroom and bathroom.

Heading back to the kitchen Sydney lay the candles and lighter on the counter and grabbed a bottle of beer from the fridge. "Want one?" Sydney gestured with the bottle.

"Sure. Got any cards? "

Cards! Perfect! "Yeah, actually, I do."

They spent the night playing a variety of card games by the fireplace, telling stories about high school, god-awful trendy hairstyles, awkward first dates, and amateur first kisses. They sounded like a couple of kids at camp. They played gin, war, and even *go fish.* Brandon reminded her how to play poker, too. When the cards played out, and the popcorn and beer were gone, they both called it a night.

Brandon made his bed out of blankets and sheets as Bailey and Baxter snuggled down together on the rocking chair. Sydney added a couple more logs to the fire, and then bid Brandon good night before retreating to her room. Brandon returned the greeting and snuggled into the cushy sofa.

Even with the fire, the sheets were ice cold as Sydney slipped underneath the covers. Shivering under the blankets she couldn't help but feel awkward with a man in the other room. Could he see her through the fire, she wondered? Was he an early riser? 'Cause she was so *not* a morning person.

As she tossed and turned trying to get comfortable, a muffled snuffling sound began emanating from the living room. It seemed Brandon was already asleep. She giggled, as she listened to him softly snore. Sydney found sleep a little harder to come by as her mind replayed the events of the day. Her last thought was if Emily was safe from the storm that night.

~ Screaming! Someone's screaming! Brandon woke up with a start. Where am I, what the? With instant clarity he recalled the storm and where he was and raced without thought into Sydney's room. Finding no intruder attacking Sydney, Brandon realized she was trapped in a nightmare.

"Sydney," Brandon shook her gently. Baxter and Bailey followed him in. Baxter pawed her bedside, whimpering.

The blood was everywhere. Sydney screamed again.

Brandon pulled her into his arms and started rocking her as he kissed her forehead, "Come on baby, wake up. It's a dream. Just a dream." The visions of blood give way as her drugged mind began to come out of the nightmare into reassuring warmth. Sobs shook her violently as her emotions were still slow to recover from the dream.

"It's okay, hon. I've got you. It was only a dream. Only a dream."

Sydney fiercely hugged him back. "It was so real," she sobbed. "There was so much blood, and I couldn't stop it. I was so terrified."

"It's over now. It's over. You're safe. There's nothing to be afraid of," he said, as he continued to rock and stroke her hair, and she continued to softly cry. "I'm right here. You don't have to be afraid anymore."

Sydney fought for control. She didn't want to be afraid anymore. She didn't want any more nightmares or to live in fear. She wanted to trust in Brandon, lean into his strength. She wanted to believe he would make it alright.

As Sydney began to calm, Brandon notched her chin up to look in her eyes and made sure she was truly out of the dreams' grip.

"I'm right, here. OK?"

"I know," she said, "I'm not afraid anymore, Brandon."

And for the first time, Sydney realized she wasn't afraid of him—of Brandon hurting her. In that moment, he saw her acceptance of him come to life, and his heart seized in his chest. She wasn't afraid of him.

Brandon kissed her then, with more love than she'd ever felt. He poured into it his reassurance that he would be there, for all her nightmares, until he'd replaced them with only happy dreams. He'd replace her haunted memories with cherished ones.

Still aware of her need to take things slowly and his desire to treat her honorably, Brandon ended the kiss quickly, as gently as he started it.

After asking if she were ok once more, and gaining an affirmative nod of her head, he lay her back down and tucked her in as if she were ten years old. She smiled at that.

"I'll be in the next room if you need me again." With one more kiss on the forehead, he bid her goodnight and shut the door.

On his way back to the sofa he put another log on the fire to keep her warm.

Lying back on the sofa he found he couldn't sleep. He was in love for sure. Unless he missed his mark, she was beginning to feel it, too.

Sydney lay in stunned silence. For once her nightmare had a happy ending. Well, sort of. Brushing her fingers across her lips she sighed and fell into a deep, dreamless sleep.

The next morning she bounded out of bed only to find Brandon gone. A note lay on top of the neatly stacked bed linen. *Tow truck called early. Couldn't bear to wake you. See you soon.* Sydney smiled. See you soon.

❧ Monday morning Sydney thought to stop by the registrar's office to ask about Emily. Maybe they could shed some light on Emily's identity. Maybe she could get an address and use the excuse of dropping off her graded papers as a chance to check up on her.

"Ms. James, can you tell me anything about this student?" Sydney asked, and handed her a post-it note. The registrar took the paper with Emily's name on it—a confused look on her face.

"She is in my first hour," Sydney explained, "and I have a paper I wish to discuss with her."

"Well, can't you just wait to see her in class?" asked Ms. James.

"She hasn't shown up yet." Sydney said, almost apologetically, realizing Ms. James might be unaware of how her hybrid classes worked.

"I don't understand, you're her teacher, aren't you?"

Richard chose right that minute to step into the room.

"What she means to say, Ms. James, is that Ms. Mackenzie here doesn't bother with traditional teaching methods, and her students don't have any requirements to come to school at all, doesn't it Ms. Mackenzie?" His nasally tenor voice made Sydney jump as he unexpectedly began speaking behind her. Sarcasm dripped from every word.

"She apparently doesn't have a clue who this young woman is."

Turning to corner Sydney, he went on, "That shouldn't surprise me with that attendance policy of yours. Why start caring now Sydney? Could it be someone is plagiarizing one of your works?"

Richard looked up at her, jutting his pointy nose in the air, daring her to defy him.

"Perhaps if you had established some *rules* for a change, for students to actually come to school for your class, you wouldn't be wasting Ms. James' time with hunting them down after the fact."

Sydney's temper flared. She'd had quite enough. As she opened her mouth to give Richard a well-deserved piece of her mind, she was beaten to it.

"Richard, kindly take your opinion and shove it," Brandon said, with a warm smile that failed to hide eyes as cold as ice.

It was Richard's turn to jump as Brandon came to Sydney's rescue. Both he and Sydney had been unaware of his presence in the hall behind them.

"The entire faculty has had quite enough of you and your opinions. In fact, if I were you, I'd think twice about harassing this young woman with your suggestions on how to run a classroom from now on. You might just be interested to know, the board of directors has not only been impressed with the performance of Sydney's hybrid classes, they have decided that the time has come to incorporate more modern teaching styles in the coming semesters. This includes, not only classes with relaxed attendance policies, but forming a committee to research and establish full online degree programs, in keeping with the larger public colleges. So, I don't know about you, but I'd imagine I'd want to get off it, and get on board with the coming changes rather than get left behind. Wouldn't you agree?"

Red faced and looking as if he would pop a vein at any moment, Richard opened his mouth several times as if to speak—giving a perfect pantomime of a hungry baby-bird. Appearing instead to think better of it, he shut his mouth, curtly nodded and left.

Ms. James smothered a smile while Sydney just stared at Richard's retreating bald head. She couldn't believe it. Did that just happen? No one had ever stood up for her like that. Ever. Not her idiot ex or even David, the one that was supposed to have really loved her. Instead of fighting back, Richard actually yielded the floor. Sydney turned her astonished gaze to Brandon.

"What?" Brandon grinned, feigning innocence. She had that proverbial deer in the headlights look, and he was trying so hard not to laugh.

"We've been sick of him for years," assured Ms. James, "just never had anyone bother to put him in his place," casting an appreciative glance in Brandon's direction. "And did you see the look on his face?" Ms. James chuckled. "Sydney, I'll see what I can find out if you can come back this afternoon."

Sydney mentally shook off the shock and returned her attention to the registrar. "Yes, thank you, Ms. James."

"The name's Marjorie, but my friends call me Madge, Sydney. Everyone does, even the students."

"Thank you, Madge," Sydney corrected herself absent mindedly, still a little in awe at what just happened.

"Well, I've got class. See you soon." With that subtle message he reminded Sydney of Sunday morning's note, and she smiled. Brandon waved to Madge on his way out, leaving Sydney still smiling, and Ms. James grinning ear-to-ear.

"I think he likes you," said Ms. James, in a hushed voice.

Sydney blushed at that—the kiss suddenly replaying itself in her mind. Sydney smiled even more. Casting a shy glance at Ms. James, Sydney just nodded as she left the office.

The daily school routine took over with, thankfully, no additional drama that day. Over the course of the afternoon the remnants of the blizzard eroded, too.

Sydney noticed over the next few days, the winter owl that nested near the garage was becoming much harder to find as the days grew longer, and more sunshine dominated the daytime hours. Spring was struggling to find its place as winter slowly lessened its grip on the landscape.

Brandon continued his daily runs with Sydney as dinner together began making its way into the routine. Each night he hugged her goodnight or placed a loving, but chaste, kiss on her lips as he left shortly after dinner. He was always the gentlemen, taking it slow. Each evening he gave her time to herself—often times leaving her wanting more.

While he knew he'd come far in gaining her trust, Brandon knew she would still need to give her time. He could tell there was something in her past that had almost broken her, and she needed time to heal—time to trust him and herself more. He was a patient man, and she was worth waiting for.

❧ March 12th arrived with a whole new set of papers. Brandon had a late appointment with a client so Sydney grabbed a burger and ate on the way home.

After letting Bax outside, she changed into her running clothes for later and decided to find Emily's paper first. Still concerned she hadn't come to class Sydney wanted to check in on her student the only way she knew how.

This assignment focused the student's attention on being descriptive in their writing. Last semester, one boy wrote such a detailed account of the step-by-step process of how to change oil in a car, Sydney was almost convinced she could do it herself after she was finished reading it.

Maybe Emily would describe something that would give Sydney a clue to how she was—where she was.

Descriptive Essay
Creative Writing
Emily Halliwell

My Shadow

I feel it on the edge of consciousness. A shadow I can see peripherally, and yet when I turn to face it, the apparition vanishes. But I know it is there—somewhat like the prickling hairs that rise on the nape of the neck when what feels like a shadow darkens the soul. I can feel it's coming, as one senses when one is being watched, yet, cannot find the intruder. It is an old friend whose acquaintance I have known all my life, coming to visit me again.

My friend has a common name, one that suggests sadness or the romantic notion of melancholy. It has an ugly side encompassing a depth of despair that few truly know, and those who do, struggle to endure. My friend's name is depression. And I will introduce it to you.

This is not its cousin, the normal type of blues or sadness that accompanies life's harsher dealings. It is not the expected visitor who comes calling when the death of a loved one is bourn on a heart filled with the pain of loss. It is not the tears that are shed when a friend leaves and your soul longs for the common ground once shared. It is not grieving for anything significant.

This is the intruder that comes when life is well and good, shoving your heart and mind into the experiences of grief and loss and hate when there is no catalyst in life to create the emotion. It is that aforementioned shadow that crosses over the sun on a glorious day that darkens the soul for no apparent reason. There is no cause for the tidal wave of emotion that chokes the life out of one's spirit. Yet, it saps one's strength nonetheless. If one is aware of it, if one has marked its passage before, they can see the signs and prepare for its coming.

If despair has a name, it is disillusionment. Its nemesis is reality. Its existence is found in the wispy fairy tale that life will have a happy ending. Its edge is that life is a lie. Its tease is the faint moments of relief. Hope that is an elusive shadow. Strength that is pretend. An emptiness that never seems filled for long. The weight of the world crushes. The proverbial one step forward and two steps back with no reward in sight.

I become sick with pain and grief of the never-ending beatings of this world. It is the blackness of it all I try so desperately to hide from that consumes me eventually, no matter how hard I fight. It grabs me, envelops me and pulls me down as I claw for solid ground. Then it releases me, leaving me shaken and spent. I fold in on my self—lost. Seeking the escape only found in sleep, where, for a time, I can lose myself in a dream world I can truly control. I am so tired of waking up every morning—so tired of going to bed alone—so tired of searching for another distraction to dull the pain. This is how it feels. It is the embodiment of death. The cruelty of it is that at least in death there is a final release.

You cannot run from it. For in running it will surely pounce upon you faster and with more devastation. It stalks the corners of your mind until weary of the chase. It is then it begins moving in for the kill. And I am finding myself oftentimes relieved that it has finally come. For the beginning of it is also its end— for now. Soon it will be over and reality will be perceived truthfully once more.

The beautiful sadness descends and manifests itself in the emotions that are so dangerously close to the surface, the tears so easily shed, the thoughts deep and profound as you ponder the darker things in life most leave untouched in their psyche, and finding solace there. Somehow by pondering the darker things, such as death and the afterlife, it brings things into focus and takes emphasis off of the moment. Facing the demon itself is a frightening and liberating thing, but face it we must. For only by facing and understanding the thing can we better prepare ourselves for the fight.

It is a liar and a thief whose whole purpose in life is to steal your joy. And logic is the only resort to making it through the onslaught of the attack. Logically, I know that depression is caused by a chemical imbalance in the brain. Much like the diabetic, whose body does not properly manufacture or control insulin, a depressed person's body cannot regulate its production of serotonin.

Serotonin is a chemical in the mind which produces a feeling of well-being— of emotional balance. Logically, I know when the darkness begins it will eventually pass, but logic and emotion are two sides of the same coin. The emotion is an overwhelming illusion masquerading as reality when despair comes on full force. And logic battles it for control. Sometimes when the attack is particularly severe, it is a conscious effort to concentrate on the reality that what you feel is not grounded—it is a powerful, very real illusion. It is tiresome.

I call it my old friend as I have made peace with it. Others are not so lucky. Some don't make it out alive. It was difficult in the beginning, when symptoms became hard to deny, admitting that I had a disorder, but like the aforementioned diabetic, it is neither something I asked for nor my fault for having. And in accepting myself as I am, I am able to overcome the social stigma that is fueled by ignorance. It is as much a part of me as the sound of my voice or the color of my eyes. It is not something I would change. To change it would alter who I am. And I like who I am. We all have our burdens to bear in life—Depression is mine.

Sydney sat there staring at the page shaking in her hand. Serotonin—it sounds benign enough. That's what they think killed David—depression. Is that what it felt like? What Emily said? A stalking pouncing darkness in the depths of despair? Oh, David. How could you not tell me? How could you live with such pain and not let me help you? Why did a stranger have to be the one to share your darkest secret?

Sydney had forgotten until that moment about what the doctor at the hospital had said. In her mind's eye, she saw as the doctor came out from behind closed doors where they'd taken David. Remembered the way he spoke to the intake nurse who then pointed her way. He approached as if in slow motion. She couldn't stand. She had to remember to breathe. He sat down in the chair in front of her.

"I am sorry. We have done all we can," he left the words hanging between them as Sydney felt her world shatter. The doctor waited a few scant moments before pressing on.

"We sent for David's records. Was he taking his medication?"

"Medication? You mean his allergy pills?" Sydney was confused. He can't be dead. He can't be. They're asking about his allergies?

"Were you aware of David's depression?"

"What depression? What do you mean? Where's David? I want to see him." She vaguely remembered stumbling over the words.

"David's physician had diagnosed him years ago. It doesn't appear he followed up with him for treatment, though. That doesn't mean he hadn't gone somewhere else. That's why I asked. Do you know if he took any medications for his depression?"

Again, no. David had no prescriptions she knew of.

"Was there a note?"

"Note? What do you mean note? Where's David? When can I see him? What note?" Why was he talking to her about a note?

"It's evident by the injuries that the wound was self-inflicted. I'm sorry, but we believe it was his intention to commit suicide."

Sydney died a thousand deaths in the single space of a heartbeat as the doctors words sunk in. No. You lie! It wasn't that! A robbery perhaps—or an accident. Not suicide! Her mind screamed as her body sat stock still—numbed and heavy, laden with shock.

The doctor could see her agony and guessed at the questions in her head.

"There was nothing you could have done." That's what the paramedic told her, too—sympathy lined his face. She'd thought at the time he'd meant that she had been too late for CPR.

What the hell did "too late" mean anyway? Was that some kind of attempt at exoneration on his part? To say to someone there was nothing you could have done? Of course, there's nothing that could be done now. Not after it was too late. Not after she'd come home with the wine for dinner to be greeted with all that blood, and the man she'd loved as the source of it. Not after she'd screamed her location into the phone to the 9-1-1 operator as his precious life's blood soaked into her jeans. Not as she vainly tried to staunch the blood that was no longer flowing. Not after.

Nothing you could have done *after,* but what about *before*? Maybe if she'd listened more, been more observant, told him she loved him more—something! What had she missed? Had he tried to tell her? Was she too caught up in her own happiness, her own success, to see that he wasn't well?

God, what is this Emily doing to her? Everyone else writes their descriptive essays on recent ski trips, their jobs, cars, boys— even one young mother wrote about her pregnancy. Who writes about this stuff?

What if, Emily? No. Sydney let the thought stop there. No. It's probably just an overreaction to the coincidence. Lots of people had depression and didn't hurt themselves or others. Even some celebrities were coming out and revealing they suffered from depression or bipolarism with no fear of repercussion. It was almost vogue in the art world to be a melancholy artiste. Emily was probably just that—some kid aspiring to cliché morbidity. What did they call them now-a-days? Goth? Emo?

Sydney put her out of her mind. No. No. No. She wouldn't relive anymore of the past tonight, and it was well past the hour of entertaining ghosts. She had to find some peace.

"Come on, boy! Let's run." Maybe if she ran fast enough, the nightmares wouldn't catch her tonight.

~ The next morning Sydney eased into the day with a leisurely bath scented with patchouli oil and lavender bath salts. Last night had been exhausting. In the end, the ghost caught up with her—fretting over Emily while she awake then stalked by nightmares while she slept. She'd finally, sometime in the middle of the night, found a way to put Emily and her pensive prose out of her mind, chalking it up to normal teenage angst. That's all it was. Thinking back, she went through many of the same depressing emotions as a teenager that was clearly evident in Emily's writing. Teenage angst does not adult depression make—not necessarily, and all she had to go on were her essays. David she knew. What did she really know about Emily? Heck, for all she knew, Emily wasn't even the author. She could be buying the essays off the Internet. Sighing at the absurdity of the thought, she put that possibility out of her mind.

Sinking further down into the tub, Sydney closed her eyes and let her mind drift to Brandon. He was definitely a more pleasant topic to consider, and certainly different from other men she'd had in her life. They enjoyed the same things, running and dogs, at least, and had some pretty similar past histories, too. He seemed to take a genuine interest in her, as well—not in controlling her, but really listening to what she had to say—encouraging her when she voiced trying new things. Lately, it seemed he was waiting on something, though. He wanted more, she could tell that, but he was holding back. Well, so was she, she realized.

He'd sounded concerned when he called to say hello last night. His session had run late, and he was beat, but he wanted to see how she was. When he asked about today, she hadn't invited him over or even mentioned getting together and claimed she had some shopping to do. She needed some space, especially this weekend, but she didn't tell him that. He mentioned he had things to do himself tomorrow and let the matter drop. She felt a little guilty about it as she closed her eyes and drew in a deep breath of the calming scents.

She must have dozed because the next thing she knew the water had turned too cool. It was time to get out of the tub and get ready to head out. Today she deserved a reward. After reading, critiquing, and grading descriptive papers about cars, fashion, and other subjects the evening before, Sydney decided she was treating herself to a trip to her favorite store. She dressed in her favorite jeans and a long sleeved tee.

Slipping into a jacket, Sydney grabbed her purse and headed for the kitchen. Baxter jumped at the sound of the keys, but Sydney soothed, "Not this time, boy." She tossed Baxter a hot dog and laughed as he trotted over to the rocker and started gnawing on the end. Satisfied he was happily occupied, she left the house.

Sydney got into her car and slowly headed for Barnes and Noble. She loved that place. They had all sorts of wonderful books, containing every imaginable plot, filling shelf after shelf after shelf. The store was nirvana, with its scents of wood polish, fresh ink, and crisp paper mingled with decadent baked goods and hot steaming coffee and tea—otherwise known as heaven to a ravenous reader like herself. There was a secret thrill Sydney felt every time she walked through the doors. It was as if she crossed the threshold into adventure and discovery, and it was about time for a new book—a new world to get lost in. That was the magic she found in reading. Anything and everything was possible.

Wandering slowly up and down the aisles, Sydney took her time picking out a book. With so many genres to choose from, it was hard to decide on which to select. Was she in the mood for a nice gothic thriller or a scorching romance? Or how about a vampire novel, she thought smiling to herself? A picture of Brandon with fangs popped into her head, and she laughed out loud at the absurdity of it. Or maybe a tale of knights in shining armor. For a brief moment Sydney imagined what Brandon would look like in armor. He'd certainly come to her rescue, hadn't he? And not just with Richard. She'd discovered from Madge that he'd even gone so far as to provide Psychology statistics to the board members in support of the online and hybrid programs she'd started—documenting how it created a healthier work and school life balance for students to have access to more flexible classes. She hadn't expected that, but she certainly appreciated it.

Ah, this is the one! Sydney's gaze was captured by a beautiful artistic rendition of a castle by a loch on the cover of a book about Medieval Scotland, circa William Wallace. A rebellious heroine and an irreverent unlikely hero—the bastard son of a ruthless Earl—must find a way to make peace within their feuding families before it kills them all. Sydney headed toward the café with her latest literary find in search of her favorite liquid indulgence—chai!

On the way to the café, she happened to notice another book on display, *Touched with Fire—Manic Depressive Illness and the Artistic Temperament*, by Kay Redfield Jamison. Ever since his death she had not forced herself to investigate the disorder that had a hand in robbing her of David. Thanks to Emily she wasn't sure if she could stop thinking about it. Perhaps if she knew more—could understand better. On impulse Sydney grabbed that one as well. Maybe she'll read it later, she thought.

After picking up her order of a hot chai tea with whipped cream and honey on top and an iced blueberry muffin, Sydney located a small table by a window in the far corner of the café. Sitting with her back to the wall, she paused and took a moment to savor the aroma of the cinnamon and honey before diving into the romance she'd just bought.

Taking a bite of her muffin, Sydney began to read. Quickly entranced, she gave herself over to the fantasy of castles, kings, earls, feuding families, and the political intrigue between Scotland and England. If she was lucky, there'd be a surprising twist at the end. She lost herself in the pleasure of sitting back and watching the scene in front of her unfold—a life that undoubtedly would have a happy ending with a lot of excitement along the way.

"Hey, stranger," came a familiar voice somewhere on the fringes of consciousness.

"HelloOOOooo."

Reluctantly dragging herself from the storyline she was immersed in, Sydney found the owner of the sing-song voice and tried to focus on his face.

Finally registering who was standing before her, she smiled, "Brandon! What are *you* doing here?"

"Picking up a new release I've been wanting to read," gesturing to his book. "How are you?"

"Fine, thank you," said Sydney, proud of herself for not betraying a hint of the slight selfish dismay she felt in not being able to return immediately to the book she had been happily lost in.

"That's good to hear. May I sit down?" gesturing at the seat in front of her.

"Yeah, sure." Sydney smiled—always the gentleman—and tucked her receipt in her book to mark her place. Oh well, she would have to wait to see how the heated battle between the main characters would turn out later.

"I'm glad I ran into you. You sounded a little down last night over the phone."

"Oh, well, you know how it is. Grading papers gets old," Sydney returned, weakly. "And I was really tired. Rewarding myself today, though!" she said, gesturing to the book she'd been reading.

"It sure *must* be a good book. I said hello three times, and it still took a few seconds for you to hear me," Brandon teased.

Blushing, she grinned, "Yeah, I do tend to get lost in them. It's my guilty pleasure. I tend to lose the ability to hear while reading. Baxter has to practically jump in my lap to get my attention. He tends to retaliate later and chew up my books if I'm not careful to put them out of his reach."

Brandon laughed at that. "At least your dog doesn't run away every chance he gets."

"HA! I've had my share of Baxter getting out, I can assure you," countered Sydney.

"So, what did you get?" Sydney gestured toward the book tucked under his arm.

"Oh, I got the new Grisham book. I love his work. This one just came out. I've been addicted to his books ever since I ran across a whole slew of them—first editions!—at an estate sale for a buck each. All hardcover, too! I couldn't pass them up. One night, I started with *A Time to Kill* and couldn't stop. I spent weeks reading everything I bought from the sale and have been hooked on his work ever since. He's great."

Sydney grinned at his boyish enthusiasm, "You garage sale? I'd never have thought. Most men I've known hate to do that."

"Well, I'll have you know I'm not *most* men." Brandon replied with a smile of his own.

Sydney smiled at that. You may be right, she thought to herself.

"You can find great stuff at a garage sale, too."

Sydney nodded as she took a sip of her Chai.

"Yuck, serious reading," Brandon teased as he picked up Sydney's other book. "*Touched with Fire— Manic Depressive Illness and the Artistic Temperament,* by Kay Redfield Jamison," he read off. "Taking an interest in psychiatry, Sydney? I'm flattered."

Sydney laughed, "Not quite, counselor, I just picked it up on an impulse."

She hesitated a moment and continued, "There was this guy I knew who was an aspiring writer, a musician, and well, I didn't know. He never told me. Now....well, it's too late. He's.... gone. I have a girl in class whose writing reminds me of his, and well, I've started to wonder. Worry."

"I'm sorry about your friend. I'm assuming he killed himself?"

At the tears that welled in Sydney's eyes he had his answer even before she wordlessly nodded and turned away. She couldn't look at him—somehow seeing his concern made it harder not to cry.

"I am deeply sorry. It is a singular tragedy for friends and family to bear that kind of loss." *This* was what had almost broken her he realized. *This* was the living nightmare that preyed upon her.

"I wish I would have known.... if only....he might not have done it if..." Sydney couldn't finish the sentence.

Brandon understood. He knew she would feel some form of misplaced blame for the death if she were a close friend of his. He knew that blame haunted her.

"For what it's worth," he continued, "I know most survivors of suicide also think 'if only,' but Sydney, once a person is really committed to suicide, there's little you can do about it. They may send out some signals initially, or they may not. With males, they're four times more likely to be successful. It's the eighth leading cause of death in the U.S. With women they're not as successful, but they try three times as often as males do."

"So tell me what's going on with this girl you mentioned? Is she openly saying she's suicidal?"

"No, she doesn't, but she writes like him. She's speaks of being depressed and being alone. I worry I'm imagining things, too, as it was two years ago that....." her voice trailed off as her composure began to slip.

Trying to reign in her emotions, she gestured she needed a moment before she could continue. This weekend was the anniversary of it all. The closer that date came, the heavier she felt the weight of David's loss. It was as clear in her memory as if it had happened yesterday.

She knew Brandon was trying to help. She'd read the same statistics before. They gave her as little comfort then as they did now. Still, Brandon was here and she knew she needed someone to talk to— someone to help figure out if Emily was in trouble, and he really seemed to want to help. She just wasn't sure where to start.

"I know people in the medical profession must hate others coming up to them asking for free advice..." Sydney began again.

"Hey, I showed up on my own, and I'm asking *you*. What gives?"

Taking a deep breath, Sydney continued.

"Emily— she's been writing these essays. I'm sure she's fine, it is just her writing is so very much like his, and the similarities scare me. She is dark, like he was, but she speaks of death as if she longs for it, and then in other papers she has written she seems fine—just lonely."

"The good thing is she knows she has it—depression, I mean. I don't want to see anything happen to Emily like what happened to my friend—to her family, if no one else realizes that she's depressed. They may not know she has it like I didn't know about my friend. So when I saw this book, well, I was just wondering how dangerous this disorder is. I bought it to try to find out if I should be worried. Is depression that dangerous, Brandon?"

"For most, it's not dangerous. People can live perfectly happy lives with it. They come up with new treatments and therapies each year, but even with advances in treatments, for some it's deadly. They may have it more severely or not know how to cope. They may not have the resources like access to ongoing medical care or the support of a loving family, et cetera, to manage the disorder successfully. Some may not know they have it at all and since they don't know, they are defenseless against it until they find out what they have and they learn how to deal with it. Those that do know may not want to deal with it either and ignore it."

"My friend knew, and that apparently wasn't enough for him."

"I know." Brandon knew he'd already told her that sometimes people don't want help. Saying it again wouldn't make it better.

Sydney watched the cars navigate around the rows of occupied spaces, looking for an open spot. Was that how David felt? Circling life? Trying to find a place to fit in with the rest? Was that what she was doing?

"So this girl, she's written something that bothers you?"

"Well, it's that she's mentioned being depressed, and some of her writings are very dark. I just thought.... Well, I don't know what I'm thinking. It was kind of an impulse buy. My first voyage into armchair psychology, I guess." Sydney laughed dryly, and took a sip of her chai. Taking her eyes off the parking lot, she returned her attention to Brandon.

"Well, here are a few things to watch out for. Does she seem depressed in person? Does she look or act dejected? What's her appearance like? Does she appear like she's not taking care of herself? Is she a healthy weight, or too large or too small? How does she interact with the other students? Any signs of self-inflicted injuries like cutting? Does she have any friends?" Brandon inquired.

"Now, if you're front-row-center to my long-running debate with Richard, you should already know I have no attendance policy. She is one of the rare few that have never shown up. So I know nothing but her name and what's in her essays. I've mentioned her in class and none of the students know her either. In fact, she's the one I was asking about in the office that day when you knocked Richard off his high horse—thanks again, by the way."

"You're welcome. Have you found out any information from Madge? Do you have an address for her?" he continued.

"No. She got back to me that same day, but with no real information—she has a PO Box for an address. No one seems to have met her, and I, well I only know her through her writings."

"How about I read her work? I'm a teacher at the university so there's no privacy violation you'd have to worry about, and at least it could set your mind at ease if you had a professional opinion on the subject."

"I think that'd be all right. In fact, since she's not come to class to pick up her graded papers I still have them all."

"How do you get them in the first place?"

"They're waiting for me in the drop box that hangs on my office door."

"Well, maybe she's one of your working students or a parent. She could have a schedule conflict and can't come to class so she drops them off. I mean, that *is* the beauty of a hybrid class."

"I tell you what. I could pick them up tonight if we go running. Or you could let me pay you back for rescuing me from Bailey the day we met and let me take you to that tavern I mentioned. They have great steaks," Brandon said, temptingly.

"Well..." Sydney hedged, "I think it would be best if I just bring them to you at school Monday. I need a little time to myself this weekend. Please understand." Oh, she hated to put him off again, but she just couldn't handle grieving around others who didn't know David. It just didn't seem right to share her private grief with an outsider.

"Fair enough." If this was the anniversary of her friend's death, he could understand her need to be alone.

"You can't say no forever," Brandon teased. "I have no classes between three and four. Does that work for you?"

"Yes, I'll be there," smiled Sydney.

"About this weekend, although you want to be alone, just remember, please," Brandon looked at her meaningfully, "I'm here if you need me."

"I know, and that means a lot. Thank you for understanding, Brandon."

"You're welcome."

⁂ At 3:15 Monday afternoon, Sydney knocked on Brandon's door. What looked like the door to another closet like her office turned out to be the entrance to a two-room office suite.

"Come on in," Brandon said, as he opened the door. As he walked back toward an adjoining room he continued, "Make yourself at home. I had an appointment run over, but I'll be done in a minute or two."

As Brandon disappeared through the door at the end of the room, Sydney surveyed her surroundings. A set of brown leather sofas sat on opposite sides of a mahogany coffee table that overflowed with popular magazines. Across from the sofas on the opposite wall, a couple of Queen Anne tapestry chairs sat opposite a matching mahogany bookcase filled with all sorts of psychiatry manuals and a few antique looking hourglasses.

The walls, she noted, were decorated with various certificates and degrees documenting his license to teach and to practice psychology. The walls were even painted! Not the battleship gray that echoed through the rest of the university, but an inviting buttery taupe. She often daydreamed about sneaking in one weekend and painting her office a different color. She would have to remember to ask him how he managed to get a nicer paint job.

From the inner room Sydney heard Brandon as he began to walk out.

"Sara, I'm glad to hear your son is feeling better. We'll figure out a way to get you caught back up on homework, so don't worry. Next time, call me ahead of time so I don't worry so much. Okay?"

"I sure will, and thanks. He'll be home from the hospital tomorrow, so I should be back in class the day after." Brandon emerged with a young woman who looked bone thin and exhausted.

As he walked Sara to the door, he continued, "Pneumonia can be rough for a little guy to get over. Take all the time you need, and don't rush back. I'm glad to hear he's coming home."

"Me, too," returned Sara, "and thanks!"

"You're welcome, and go get some rest!"

"I'll try," said Sara, as she disappeared into the hall.

Brandon waved good-bye to Sara, then turned a welcoming smile on Sydney as he shut the door.

"Wow, this is very nice. How'd you manage to get so lucky?" Sydney said, as she continued to walk around the room. Sticking her head inside to peek at Brandon's inner office she found another large room with similar furnishings.

"This place is four times the size of my office."

"Well, they were gracious with my accommodations since I see students pro bono and need the privacy. There are many tenured staff members that weren't too thrilled when I got this one, I can assure you. This is the outer office—kind of like a waiting room. If I need to talk to a student on a more personal issue, I have this back office for more privacy," gesturing to the back room.

Brandon walked toward the sofa set, signaling Sydney to join him.

"I guess I can see why you'd need it, but that sure doesn't make my office any easier to live with after seeing this," Sydney joked. "Anyway, thanks for your help. Here's what I have so far." Sydney handed Brandon the papers as they were seated.

"No thanks are necessary, it's my pleasure." Brandon took the papers from Sydney as she sat on one sofa and set them on the table as he took a seat across from her. "Before I start reading, what information do you have on her?"

"Her name is Emily Halliwell." Sydney began, "The registrar has a PO Box in town, but no physical address. Her birthday is Christmas day, and she's 25 years old. She was a transfer from another rural college; however, I contacted them, and they don't have any more information than we do. She had a PO Box there, as well."

"She did attend her classes in person when she was enrolled in school there, and the teachers remembered her as a small blonde who was quiet, yet friendly. She was pretty, but shy, and didn't really socialize with many people."

"She came to class, had average to above average grades and left last semester. No one seems to know anything other than that. No one knew of a job or family or anything. There was no one listed as an emergency contact, either."

"Oh, and another odd thing. She paid for her books and tuition in cash. There's not even a credit card number to track her down with."

"My class is the only one she's enrolled in at our university. The guidance counselor said with this class she graduates. If she doesn't come to graduation, we'll have no other way to find her."

"She spent three plus years there and wanted to come here to graduate?" mused Brandon. "Wonder if it's the university name she wanted on her diploma, maybe for a particular job or sentimental reason? Or her family could have moved. That could be why she's so sad. Maybe she left to come here due to some other reason, like an unexpected pregnancy she wants to hide. That still happens in the more religious families, even in this day and age."

"I'm glad I'm not the only one with an overactive imagination." Sydney teased. "Who knows? It's just odd. With David..." Sydney stopped short at hearing herself say his name out loud for the first time since his funeral.

"Is that him? Is that the friend who died?" Brandon softly asked.

Sydney took a deep breath, "Yes. David." There it was again. His face—those eyes—that smile—her ghost. This time, though, it wasn't such an overwhelming agony. This time, it wasn't so bad.

Taking another deep breath, she began again.

"David was my friend, yes—and my fiancé."

Brandon suspected as much, but the revelation still sucker punched him in the gut. He smiled at Sydney, hiding his reaction. It wouldn't do for her to know he'd come to care for her so much that he felt jealous of a dead man.

"He was an aspiring author. A musician, too. He played piano. He was so very full of life. He seemed genuinely happy most of the time. He seemed just like everyone else. Apparently, he suffered from depression. I never knew about it. I've often wondered why he didn't tell me. Was he ashamed? Could he not accept it? Or did he reject the diagnosis altogether?"

"It's not like he was never down. Everyone gets down from time to time. I always thought his darker writings were just the way he wrote. Like a gothic novelist. That's one of the things that got to him the most— being rejected as an author. You know how hard it is trying to get published, trying to get work, especially when you're just starting out? The industry can be unkind, even brutal. He got frustrated with that at times. I'm sure it didn't help that I was already an established writer and working rather steadily when we met, but he seemed to take it all in stride, like it was no big deal."

"I had no clue he had a disorder. The ER doc said it was in his records, but we never spoke of it. I'm not sure if he believed he had a disability or not— but, if I'd have only known I would have tried harder to save him."

"Can you tell me what happened? It usually helps to talk about it, if you're up to it." Brandon gently urged. Let me share your burden, Brandon thought to himself. Let me in Sydney. Let me be there for you.

Sydney sighed. It was time. She had to face it.

"I was coming home from a conference. I called David that morning before the final lectures began. I told him about the lectures I'd already given and how well they'd been received. I rambled on excitedly about an idea I had for a new short story that I was intending to pitch to a literary magazine. I remember he liked the idea."

"I asked how he'd been and what he was doing. He said he was completely moved into my duplex, but hadn't gotten around to unpacking. David and I were to be married in a week, so he'd moved in during the week I was away at the conference. I had the bigger place."

"He was planning dinner for when I got home later that night, and he rattled off what we were going to have—Bourbon Glazed Salmon and grilled vegetables on a bed of long-grained wild rice. Did I mention he was a fantastic cook? He was *so* good. I think he could have made a go of it as a chef if he'd wanted to."

"He said he'd picked up a fifth of Bourbon for the salmon, but didn't realize we were low on wine. He asked me if I would mind picking up a bottle after my flight. It was a short flight home, and my car was at the airport, so I assured him I didn't mind."

"When I look back on it, I remember he seemed fine, but not as excited as I'd have thought he would be about the success of the conference or my return home—or even our upcoming marriage. I thought he just sounded very tired. He'd often had trouble sleeping so I really didn't think much of it, and my mind was buzzing with all the last minute thoughts on the lectures ahead. So I just dismissed his less-than-chipper tone and went right on talking."

"I had no clue he was planning his own death. I wonder if he did when he was talking to me. If he was leading me to believe things were fine. If he was sitting there with the loaded gun in his hand the whole time we were talking—staring down the barrel—working up the courage." Sydney shuddered as her mind envisioned her own words. David—in her mind's eye as she had found him that day.

He would have been sitting on the sofa in his favorite old blue jeans that had been washed so many times they were a faint baby blue and threadbare in spots. He wore no shoes—his bare feet, long with elegant bones and slender straight toes. She always thought he had beautiful feet, like in the renaissance oils of the crucifixion—the feet of Christ—their delicate beauty impaled by a cruel spike. At least His death meant something.

David wore a button down oxford rolled up at the sleeves to just below the elbow. His legs were carelessly sprawled as he slumped down in the cushions. One shoulder notched up holding the phone to his ear, commenting in the appropriate places of the conversation, while both hands slowly rotated the gun—inspecting the barrel—inserting the clip—chambering a round. God, she had to stop this!

"I didn't even know he owned a gun. I've turned this over and over in my head re-playing every little thing we said that day and all the months before. I find nothing that stands out— no warning."

Sydney looked at Brandon then. "Why couldn't he tell me? Why didn't he let me know, let me help?" He shook his head.

She hadn't expected an answer. She knew only God knew the answer to that question—a God that she hadn't spoken to since that day. A different grief assailed her as she realized she needed to get right with God, too. Forgive me, she prayed. I'm trying, she implored.

She sighed and stared at the bookcase as she found her place again in the story.

"Anyway, when I got to the lecture hall I found out my last few lectures were cancelled. A pipe broke in the hall. Or was it the bathroom next door? Something like that. I can't remember exactly. Whatever the reason, the floor was flooded, and there were no halls available to move the lectures to. I'd already checked out of the hotel, and my bags were loaded in the rental car, so I decided to surprise David by grabbing an earlier flight back. I couldn't wait to get home and tell him more about how fantastic the conference had been—to see him again."

"I got in town just after noon rather than at 7 that night, like he'd expected. I decided to pick up some champagne, as well as the wine he'd asked me to get for dinner, so I headed to Mike's Liquor Store. We always went there. Mike and I had known each other forever—all the way back to high school."

"After making my selections, I stayed awhile chatting with him. His wife had just had their first baby so he just had to show me the little guy's pictures, and he couldn't stop relating all the details of the delivery—how cool it had been, but at the same time how gross it was. The joy *and* the terror. I laughed at that. He went on relating how little sleep he'd been getting. Then beamed about how his wife was still glowing. He was so proud of her. I remembered thinking that I was looking forward to being that happily married, maybe having a kid someday."

"I couldn't help but chat a little about how the conference went and about how things were going in general with work. We discussed the upcoming wedding. Mike was catering the liquor for the rehearsal dinner and the open bar at the reception. He had a new organic variety he wanted me to consider. I'd bought it for dinner that night."

"Maybe if I'd not stayed to chat with him, maybe if I'd gone straight home, maybe I'd have gotten home in time, and we could have talked it out. Or maybe I should have insisted David come with me to the conference. I don't know."

She looked again at Brandon.

Brandon could see how helpless she felt. He shook his head from side to side in empathy and waited for Sydney to finish. It wouldn't help her at this moment to tell her she was wrong and to not blame herself. She had to say out loud what happened next, and they both knew it. So he waited. He prayed.

Sydney sighed, she knew what was coming. She knew what she had to say. She would get through this. Staring unseeing at the bookcase again she sorted out what to say next, stalled for a little more time. She didn't want Brandon to see her cry. Again.

She looked so bone weary and fragile, Brandon wanted to scoop her into his lap and hold her. Knowing she needed to do this though, he waited for her to organize her thoughts and gather her strength, while he resisted the urge to stop her from re-living the unimaginable.

"Anyway, after picking up the White Zinfandel and the champagne, I drove to the bakery for some strawberry pie—his favorite. I finally headed for home around 3pm. I walked in my front door and called out a greeting. No one answered my call. There were no sounds of life—no TV, radio, or even smells of recent cooking. Nothing. I walked into the living room."

Sydney stopped to choke back a sob as her gaze focused sightlessly on the floor beneath her feet. It was clearly visible on her face that her mind's eye was reliving the scene. She no longer saw buttery taupe walls or brown leather sofas. There was no beautiful rug at her feet. She was in her home in Texas staring death in the face.

Brandon was already around the coffee table crouching protectively in front of her, not touching her, but looking as if he was about to pounce on anything that would try to hurt her and tear it to shreds. He captured and held her gaze to draw her out of the past she was reliving in her mind and back to the present.

"You were the one who found him." The words gentled by his tone scarcely altered the harrowing fact. Brandon tasted the bile that rose in his throat at the very thought.

Tears began streaming silently down her face as Sydney focused on his eyes—his beautiful whisky colored eyes. She grasped at the strength reflected in the amber depths and willed her own resolve to rise in response. She would finish this—she was determined to exorcize the ghost who had followed her here.

"There was blood all over the place—splattered from the gunshot wound to his head. I was standing in a pool of his blood. I realized I was screaming. I dropped the wine, champagne and the pie. The wine bottle shattered—the sound, like a gunshot registering to my mind what had happened here."

"I remember how the box fell open, as it too hit the ground, and the strawberries from the pie bounced out of the box into the puddle on the floor—the glaze was almost the same color as the blood. I noticed also how macabre the strawberries looked too, like chunks of brain matter or something like that. It was too surreal. Who *thinks* these things in that millisecond of time while someone they love lay dying?"

"I fell to my knees franticly calling his name. His blood soaked through my jeans, still warm, and I kept thinking, still warm, still time, still warm, still time."

"I ripped my cell phone out of my back pocket, called 9-1-1, and frantically relayed the address, begging them to hurry as I grabbed a throw blanket off the nearby chair and held it to his head where all the blood was. I braced my knees around his head to hold the blanket in place and started CPR compressions."

"I told him it would be all right. Help was on the way. Brandon, I even cursed at him, 'hold on damn it, don't you leave me!'"

"I think I threatened him. I know I begged. I told him to hold on. I told him I loved him. I never told him good-bye. Just to stay with me. Everything would be ok."

"The paramedics got there in minutes. We raced against hope to the hospital. It was too late. I don't know how long they worked on him—less than an hour. In retrospect, I have the feeling he was too far gone by the time I got home."

"Since David had indicated on his driver's license that he was an organ donor the ER summoned his medical records. The doctor asked me if I knew about his depression when he came out to deliver the news."

"I didn't even know. How could I not know? How could he never tell me? There was no note, no explanation, no reason or even an apology. He didn't say good-bye, and I never had a chance to stop him. It's not fair! I don't want this to happen to someone else. No one should have to survive a loved one's suicide." She looked intently at Brandon still crouched in front of her. "No one."

"Sydney."

She sightlessly stared at him. He wondered if she breathed.

"What happened next?"

The plaster mask that had been her face broke again at the memory. Tears flooded in, cascaded—relentless. Through broken sobs and deep shuddering breaths the aftermath poured out.

"I had to call his parents. At first, they said I'd always be their daughter, even though David and I hadn't been married, yet. They told me that we'd get through this together no matter what, but, by the time we laid David to rest, they hated me. Somehow, it was if I had pulled the trigger and murdered their son."

"Then Chloe died, and I had to bury her on my own, in the backyard— all by myself. I didn't even own a shovel, for crying out loud, and had to go to the hardware store to buy one. The cashier must have thought I was crazy. All I could say was 'my cat,' but he still just stared. It seemed for weeks I'd find her toys hidden in the couch, under a chair, behind the TV, or under the bed, and I relived her death, and then his death, all over again. It's like she couldn't live without him, and she did what I could not. She died right along with him."

"I miss how she'd creep up at night and lie across my throat, purring, and fall asleep until morning. I was ashamed at how many times I had gotten annoyed with her in the past when it seemed that she only wanted me to pet her when I was working—trying to supplant my laptop from my lap to get my attention. I felt selfish about the times I'd ignored her and shooed her off. It made me feel that somehow I was partly responsible for her death, too."

"Then Todd and Sharon divorced—those were his parents, my future parents-in-law. I guess they couldn't cope. The fighting over who was to blame for not seeing it, not knowing, tore them apart. The blame game, I guess. It happened so fast. After they filed they sent their divorce attorney to pick up David's personal belongings. I never heard from them again, and I was alone. Again."

"I couldn't stand my own home. He'd not even lived there, and most of the things were mine, his college bachelor pad being such as it was, but he'd filled the house with me—with our memories. And it all became more like a memorial mausoleum to the dead."

Sydney stood and paced the room.

"This chair," she motioned to an empty space in his office, "on this end of the dining room table, was where David sat when he ate dinner." She walked in an oval shape seeing images of her past. Turning, she motioned again, "This end of the sofa was his when we watched movies together."

Pointing, "That coaster on the end table—he never used it, but that was his, too." Staring, she continued, "I was constantly wiping up the condensation rings to preserve the wood finish, but I didn't care. He wasn't intentionally cruel or mean in his thoughtlessness—just absentminded, as if he forgot those mundane cautions, his mind on more important things."

Brandon tried to fill in the blanks of her home as her mind mapped them for him by her gestures.

Sydney turned back to him again as if remembering he was there, and where she was, but her emotional self was still in her old home while her physical body anchored focus back to Brandon.

"The third rung of the front hall coat rack—his. The right hand side of the toothbrush holder—his. I found myself unable to remove the toothbrush, or hang anything on the third hook, or use the coasters, sit in his chair or on the sofa. There was too much, and what was me of the house was somehow gone."

"I sold it all. I took only my clothes and few personal effects that had no ties to David, and I left. There were too many ghosts. For a while, I felt they wanted to kill me, too."

She looked away then. Shame, embarrassment, honesty filled the next words she spoke. "And I wasn't sure I didn't want to go. I mean. I didn't want to take my own life, but if God—a God I haven't been able to speak to much since then either—but He who had not stopped David from leaving— if He wanted to have mercy on me and take me, too, I would have really been OK with that."

Looking shyly back, a half a smile formed as she continued, "I know that sounds crazy, and I don't want to die, Brandon, so please don't worry. I think it was just that *place*. I just couldn't breathe, couldn't live there anymore."

Even in her grief she was comforting him that she didn't want to kill herself so he wouldn't worry. Even here she is thinking of others, Brandon noted. His pride in her notched up that much more.

A heavy sigh brought her back to the moment fully. Relieved, she shut the door on the past. This time, she almost heard an audible click. Returning to the couch, she sat in front of Brandon.

"I see something of David in Emily, Brandon. In her writing. I feel like maybe I was given a second chance with her. Like maybe his death won't be in vain if, through it, I can save her. David's life can't have been for nothing, Brandon."

Brandon gently touched her then. He eased onto the sofa next to her and tenderly held her close as she softly cried out the rest of her grief. She cried for David, for Chloe the cat, the future in-laws and their shattered dreams, her lost home and fractured future—trying to say good-bye to someone she wasn't sure how to let go of.

He knew. He understood.

She wrapped her arms around him and held tight. She'd done it. She'd told someone. Instead of feeling the shards of memory piercing her heart and trying to shred her into pieces, she felt the faint whisper of release. She felt, for the first time in a long time, truly safe. Safe from her ghosts. The pain was still there, but she felt less swallowed up in it, less ravaged by it.

Brandon was so proud of her. She'd trusted him with David—with her pain and insecurity—with her darkest thoughts and deepest regret. More importantly, she'd trusted herself. She'd found the strength to face her past. How brave she'd been in the face of that horror. How alone she must have felt all this time.

He could tell she had loved David and loved him deeply. It made his heart ache for her—to see and feel her pain and loss. He grieved for himself, too. That a woman had yet to love him as deeply as Sydney had obviously loved her fiancé, and he ached all the more for her, knowing that somehow it made her loss all the more bitter. That by taking his own life David had betrayed her more than his own wife and friend betrayed him. He knew firsthand how it felt to be betrayed—but the betrayal she felt was certainly worse than what his wife and best friend had done to him. In ways he couldn't begin to imagine.

Suicide is the ultimate selfish betrayal for the ones that are left behind, even if the suicidal person doesn't realize it. More often than not, they fail to see through their own pain to grasp what they're doing, or will be doing to others. Brandon knew that. Still, that didn't stop him from wishing David was still alive so he could break his neck.

⁂ Sydney sat there relieved to finally have it all out. Easing out of Brandon's embrace she found concern etched all over his face.

"I will read the essays on one condition," he said, looking down at her with a stern frown.

Sydney looked at him with a start. One condition, she thought angrily? How dare he? Pulling away from him—ice fill her voice. "And that is?"

"You let me take you out of here and cheer you up— Doctor's orders," Brandon soothed. He smiled slightly and cocked an eyebrow at her, daring her to say no. When she just sat there and looked at him in shock he took advantage of her silence. "You can't stay locked away forever. It was not your fault, Sydney. Do you hear me? Some people don't want to be saved."

"David had a lot to live for. He was going to marry a successful, beautiful woman."

He noted with curiosity that Sydney winced. Didn't she know she was a knock-out? That she was amazing?

"No, don't do that," seeing her recoil at his praise. "You are, and he knew it. A blind man would know it. You're kind, thoughtful, creative and considerate, too. Not to mention smart!"

"He had a lot to live for, as well. You say he was attractive? A good cook, a musician and a writer, too? He had a good life had he wanted it. For whatever reason, he had a deep hidden pain and made an awful choice. He could have chosen to get help. He could have chosen to work through whatever it was with you, by your side, and make the happily-ever-after happen, but, he let it go. He didn't choose to get help from his parents or you. He chose to die.

HE chose, Sydney. Not you." I would have chosen you, Brandon thought to himself. In a heartbeat.

The doubt still showed clearly on her face. Brandon pressed on. She needed to see this from a different point of view. She was slowly dying inside over something she had no real control over.

"Did you ever stop to think that by entering into a relationship you might have initially saved him? But in doing so, you also denied him that choice of ending it all and stopping the pain? I heard in a movie, or read somewhere, that the depressed person experiences a true moment of happiness when they choose to end it all. They feel a powerful release in the decision. Not that it's right or fair, but some do."

"Maybe he didn't resent your success. Maybe what he resented was you giving him a hope—a will to live when his will to die was just a little bit stronger. Living is so much harder than giving up. Dying is the easiest choice of them all, and you stole the ease of that choice from him with love. Maybe he didn't want to hurt you—that in truly loving you, in his mind, he decided to kill himself while you were away, hoping someone else would find him first. That he felt, with his depression that he'd someday hurt you enough to lose you anyway. Your relationship with him, in his mind, delayed the inevitable. For surely, had he wanted to live, he would have fought for it—for life—for you."

"Whatever emotional pain, personal torment, guilt or obsession he had, he just couldn't find the strength, and love turned to resentment, hope in a new life to anger, anger to despair and despair to suicide."

"For some people, they're only comfortable with pain. They're not sure how to be happy. They're only consoled when they can bring others down with them. You couldn't go down to his level. He couldn't stay at yours, and he chose not to stay at all."

"How do you know it's not me? That I didn't push him away? Why did his parents abandon me, too? If you're right, they had to know he was like that—had to have some idea? Why blame me?" Sydney demanded.

"Perhaps you were their last hope. He seemed happy with you. Parents don't always realize that they can do their job well and their child still can grow up and have problems that the parents didn't create and can't address—or worse, they can't fix. Perhaps they were able to exonerate themselves in what they considered their failure to help their son. So they pinned all their hopes on you. As if your success would prove they hadn't really failed, after all."

"When you failed," Sydney started at that, betrayal showing clearly on her face. "When their *perception* of you failing culminated in the death of their son," Brandon clarified, "they couldn't accept that it was their beloved son's fault any more than they could cope with their own helplessness in saving him. Don't you see? You became the failure, a scapegoat, so they could find a way to go on with less shame and less pain. Their coping mechanism became an instrument of your self-torture. Although, it sounds like it didn't work for them for long, and they turned on each other too, in the end."

"Sydney, it was wrong of them to blame you. Just as wrong of them to do to you as it was for David to do what he did to you all. Yet, it allowed them their grasp at happiness. They just probably didn't realize what they're doing because they couldn't see through their own pain any more than he could."

"You were stronger than them all. You beat this. You survived even with your ghosts and continued to improve your life while battling your past. Do you not see how amazing that is? How amazing you are?"

"In doing so, you're here to help Emily, if she's able to accept your help. And you have me. You're not facing the ghosts alone any longer, Sydney."

Before she could voice the protest forming on her lips, he continued, "I understand how you feel—wondering if you'd gotten home earlier, and asking yourself if you had, would he be with you today. You have to stop doing that to yourself. Maybe, it would have stopped David *that* day if you *had* arrived earlier, but there would have been nothing you could have done to stop him the next time he decided to end it. Nothing. No more than if I had come home earlier that day would I have stopped my wife from having an affair or would have been able to save my marriage once she decided to leave. You can love someone with all you have and things still not work out. I'm sure you'll come to accept that with time—even if you don't think so now."

"I also understand the need to be alone for a while. To heal. Eventually, you are going to have to rejoin the human race. You're not really living life by shutting yourself away and not taking chances on being hurt again. I know. I've been there. You have to start living again."

"All I'm asking for is to go out with me and have some fun." Brandon quietly said.

Sydney struggled with wanting to say yes and wanting to say no. Something deep inside her knew he was right. David chose—she didn't have a choice then, but she did now.

Dinner sounded harmless enough, but she knew this was more than that—he was asking her out on a date—to accept more than just his friendship. Because that's where she knew this was going with Brandon. The dinners at her place and running together had broken through her isolation. The kiss the night of the nightmare opened her heart enough that she had learned to feel safe with him. And she continued to feel safe. Safe enough to let him in a little more each day, bit by bit. His patience gave her time—was giving her time—to heal and get to know him, she realized, in an unthreatening way, with no pressure.

This was a date. An official step. It was a declaration that this was more than just friends. Her saying yes meant she had to be fair to Brandon, too. To give him the chance he deserved in her life. She liked Brandon. No, like wasn't the right word. It was much more than that. She cared for him. She was terrified to admit it, but she wanted more, too. Brandon watched her mull it over. Take a chance on me, he prayed.

"Yes, Brandon," she smiled, as she made up her mind. "I'm not promising I'll be the best of company, especially tonight, but yes. You're the first person I've told anything to, other than the police and the doctors. Surprisingly, I feel a bit relieved to have finally told someone the whole story. And Brandon, I really appreciate you being there—and not just today."

"Great! I hoped you would agree." Brandon tucked Emily's papers into his computer bag. "I appreciate you trusting me enough to let me hear your story, too, but enough of the past, and that goes for both of us. Let's go have some fun. If we drop your car off on the way, you won't have to worry about it. I'll be the designated driver!"

Smiling, Sydney agreed.

⁂ On the drive home, Sydney felt as if a weight had been lifted from her heart, at least to a large extent. She'd never thought about the simple fact that even if she had been home earlier, or taken David with her to the conference, that he still could have chosen to end his life another time. What if she was the reason he had not taken his own life at an earlier date like Brandon said? What if she had bought him the time he had from when she met him until he gave up? Bought him time where he could have found help or faith or hope? It could have been worse—maybe the scene could have played out down the road when they had kids. Oh, God, she couldn't imagine a child finding their father like that.

She thought again about the timing. Shouldn't getting married be the happiest time of their lives? A new thought emerged. Perhaps he was overwhelmed by the marriage. Maybe he realized that if they lived together she'd find out about his depression. Openness and honesty. Lies and cover-ups. Wasn't that what Emily had said? Could he have been worried she'd reject him over it? His not telling her indicated he had been keeping things from her—his future wife. Would that have been any way to start a marriage? There must have been some truth to it since he hadn't told her. It was beyond her how he could have thought she'd reject him, if that had been the case. They could have worked it out. God would have been there for them both. God had been there all along, she realized.

Brandon met Sydney at her cabin after checking in on Bailey. He played with Baxter while she freshened up her make-up and tried to figure out what to wear.

Sydney was not sure deciding what to wear was the problem. It was more of a definite shortage of wardrobe. As she listened to Brandon and Baxter play, she looked through her closet. Maybe she did need to start living again, but, she had better do some shopping first if she was going to get out more. Between work attire and work out clothing she had little in the way of a casual wardrobe. Luckily, she did have a good pair of jeans and a cable knit sweater that wasn't too casual. Her old Doc Martens she used to go hiking in looked just decent enough to go with the ensemble.

Taking a quick look in the mirror she decided her makeup looked as good as it was going to get and pulled her hair back into a ponytail with a clip. Time to go, she said to herself as she tried to ignore the slightly sick sensation growing in her stomach.

Brandon helped her into her coat and gently pulled her ponytail out for her.

Sydney grinned at his thoughtfulness.

She paused to grab a treat out of the kitchen for her buddy, and tossed Baxter a Milk Bone. Thus appeased at being left behind, he trotted off to the rocker with his atonement.

"Hungry?" Brandon asked, as he held open the door for her.

"Yeah," Sydney replied, and turned to lock her door behind her.

As they headed back out into the frosty night air, Brandon noticed Sydney seemed a little more at peace, but shadows still haunted her eyes. He was going to do his best to erase those.

He meant what he'd told her. She deserved to be happy— have a little fun. He was starting to wonder if she suspected he intended to apply for the job, and for more than just tonight.

~ Brandon took Sydney to a small pub and grill. It was actually a renovated Victorian home someone had lovingly turned into a restaurant. It had a quaint wood shingle roof trimmed in burgundy and wood siding painted hunter green. The front and left hand side of the building was skirted by a large deck filled with tables for outdoor dining. She could imagine it'd be a popular place in the warmer months.

They arrived early for dinner. Brandon hoped there wouldn't be much of a wait. As they walked up the broad wooden stairway to the empty outdoor deck, a squirrel bounced down the walkway ahead of them as if showing them the way. Brandon opened the glass door for Sydney.

Inside what was once the foyer, there was a wooden hostess stand that reminded her of a pulpit. Hugging the walls were two wooden benches which looked suspiciously like repurposed pews. She wondered if there was a hymnal rack on the back. The daily special was spelled out on a black chalkboard in colorful chalk—Shepherd's Pie. Sydney almost laughed at the coincidence.

Looking around though, the pastoral imagery gave way to Victorian charm. Every nook and cranny had antique accents to enhance the old world ambiance. A side table held a pair of Victorian ceramic figurines painted in soft pastels and gold gilt trim, a hand crocheted doily underneath, the kind made by a loving hand rather than a machine. Above it was a brick-a-brack shelf holding sets of tea cups and saucers, each hand painted with different types of flowers.

Just beyond the hostess stand, the central focal point of the main dining room was an enormous cherry wood bar—complete with a brass foot railing around the base and padded brass bar railing above. Matching brass barstools lined the rails. There wasn't a spittoon, but it certainly would have fit in. The bar kind of reminded her of the one on the TV show Cheers, if the one on the show had been backed up to a huge mirror on one side. The mirror was etched with filigree borders and framed in mahogany to match the bar. Every imaginable bottle of liquor was housed on the shelves on each side of the mirror while every pub glass required for the various drinks they served hung underneath the liquor shelves, ready to be filled.

Near the hostess station was a huge fireplace with a dancing fire, perfect for newly arrived guests to warm themselves by while they waited to be seated. Sydney walked over to it and warmed her hands. The fireplace had an old-fashioned iron arm with a cast iron kettle perched on the end, dangling near the fire. From inside the simmering pot came the scents of apple, cinnamon, and citrus wafting out to greet her.

An equally bubbly hostess arrived and took them to their table. As they followed her through the tavern, the scents of roasted chicken, grilled steak, and other savory dishes greeted them. The air was filled with the aromas of rich sauces, aromatic roasted potatoes, and fresh baked herb-bread. Sydney realized how hungry she had become and was instantly glad she'd decided to come.

The hostess motioned them to a booth set inside a secluded alcove. The room was skirted with similar compartments. To sit down, one had to step up into the horseshoe shaped landing into a partially secluded booth. Even illuminated with two wall sconces and a small oil lamp burning on top of the lace edged table cloth, the space was scantily lit and best suited for lovers rather than a couple of teachers out for a bite to eat—even if it was a real date.

It even had curtains across the front of the table, pulled back with ties, but still blocking most of the rest of the dining room floor. Sydney cocked her eyebrow at him in mock suspicion.

"I swear, I had nothing to do with it!" Brandon defended himself, laughingly, after seeing Sydney's look.

Noting Sydney's hesitance, the confused hostess replied, "This is all we have ma'am, the other wait staff haven't arrived yet, so the other sections are still being restocked and cleaned for tonight's service. They haven't opened up, yet. Would you like to wait until another table comes available? I'm sure it wouldn't take too long."

"No. Thank you, it's lovely," Sydney smiled reassuringly at her.

Brandon held aside the curtain so she could climb into the alcove.

"Well, I'm sorry for making you feel uncomfortable..." he started to say.

"No really, it's charming. Just not what I was expecting."

"Me, either, but you have to admit it is cozy." He laughed more as she pulled a face at him.

"Your waitress should arrive shortly. May I get you some drinks to get you started while you look over the menu? Beer, wine, tea?" asked the hostess.

"I'll have a glass of Riesling." Sydney replied. "Oh, and a glass of water, too, please."

"I'll take water, too, and a beer. What do you have on tap?" asked Brandon.

After selecting a Killian's Red from the list the hostess rambled off, they both silently studied the menu.

"Have you been here before, Brandon?"

"Only a few times? Why?"

"I wondered if you had any recommendations."

"Well the steak is delicious—aged to perfection and melts like butter in your mouth," he grinned, "and the Pasta Primavera is very good, too. Let's see, I didn't care for the Bourbon Glazed Salmon, though..." Brandon looked up as he realized what he'd said. He grimaced at his own slip up.

Sydney's eyes were glued to the menu as if she hadn't heard, but her face had turned as white as the tablecloth. "Go on," she said, knowing full well Brandon hadn't meant anything by it.

"Ah, ahem," he cleared his throat, taking her prompt to move on and hastily continued, "well, the Fettuccini Alfredo is a little too rich for my taste, but I highly recommend the Coconut Shrimp. It's to die for!" Brandon froze, not believing he'd stuck his foot in his mouth twice! And in such rapid succession, too!

Sydney immediately looked up in disbelief at his horrid choice of words, but after seeing Brandon's face, she slowly began to laugh. Brandon looked as if he'd swallowed a bug, and *that* bug was trying to crawl its way out again.

With that thought, the giggles began en force, as the unreality of it all wore off. Brandon turned a deeper shade of red which only made it worse.

"Oh, Brandon, stop trying so hard!"

Brandon began to laugh too, "I am so sorry, I can't believe my mouth tonight."

"Really, it's ok." Tears started streaming out the corners of her eyes as her laughter continued.

Relieved and amused, he watched Sydney succumb to a full blown case of the giggles. All he could do was sit back, smile, and enjoy watching her laugh at his expense—all the while thanking heaven his foot-in-his-mouth faux pas had somehow managed to cheer her up. Finally!

"Welcome to McPhee's Landing. My name is Tiffany, and I'll be your waitress. Here are the drinks you ordered," she said, eyeing the grown woman that was still giggling like a five year old as she set the drinks on the table alongside a basket of bread and butter. "Are you two ready to order?"

"Oh, yes," Sydney gained a little composure, "I'll have the Coconut Shrimp. I hear it's to die for!" With that, she collapsed back into a fit of laughter.

"Me, too," Brandon laughed, handing the waitress their menus. "I'm going down with the ship anyway."

"So much for suave and debonair," Brandon laughed.

"Oh yes, very smooth, counselor. Is that how you break all your patients out of their doldrums, by tripping all over yourself?"

Using his best imitation of a British Professor, Brandon quipped, "Quite so, I find the ego deflation to be most effective—right alongside the foot-in-the-mouth maneuver. Very efficient indeed."

"Indeed," mimicked Sydney.

"So, how long have you been teaching?" Sydney decided to let him off the hook.

"Going on five years now, I think, but less than a year here," replied Brandon, relaxing into the evening.

"Really, and is Psychology the only class you teach?"

"Since going back into part-time practice, yes. I've taught a little Sociology and History, too."

"You indicated you weren't always a teacher. You said you were a writer? What kind of writing did you do?" Brandon asked, as he grabbed a knife and the honey-butter and selected a croissant. When he'd buttered two, he handed one to Sydney.

"Thanks," Sydney said, taking the bread.

"I used to be a freelance writer although, I originally started school to become a teacher. I've done some work for magazines, newspapers, and written some short stories. Mostly, once the writing took off, I got onto a writer's conference circuit making speeches on how to write, how to get started, how to write better—you know, things like that. I wonder, in retrospect, if that was another thing that bothered David. I mean, here he is unsuccessfully trying to get started, and I was touring the country being paid to teach people how to do just that. Huh," Sydney sat there for a moment thinking, "It's not like I didn't give him tips and such, but I never thought of that before. Maybe it affected him more than he let on."

"And now you teach college kids the fundamentals of creative writing?" Brandon redirected—happy, at least her comment sounded more speculative than guilt-ridden at her own success.

"I love interacting with the students, so it seemed a natural transition. When I was first in college, I studied for a degree in education. Then I segued over to journalism, and I abandoned the idea of becoming a teacher at that time, although I graduated with a degree in both. I'd come too far in education before switching to journalism to not go ahead and complete both degrees."

"When everything happened, I decided to just take a step back. My inheritance, while sufficient for a time, wouldn't last forever, and I had to eat, as they say, so I revisited the idea of teaching. So, here I am, making a new start."

Tiffany arrived with the food and sat each dish on the table. "Would you like more to drink?"

"Sure, I'll have just one more glass. Brandon?"

"Why not?"

The Coconut Shrimp smelled heavenly. Sydney took a bite. She couldn't stifle a moan at how delicious the buttery sweet crust and succulent shrimp tasted. Brandon smiled at her reaction. He was well aware of how decadent the shrimp was.

"That's sort of what happened to me, too—falling back on teaching, that is. When Jennifer, that was my wife's name, when she destroyed our marriage, it seemed too risky to deal with other vulnerable people while I was coping with my own personal crisis. Teaching the aesthetics of psychology was almost a rote exercise, so it was like going on autopilot. It let me heal while going on with my life, until I could make a new beginning."

"I hear that!" Sydney agreed around a mouthful of shrimp.

Tiffany returned with their new drinks. Brandon held his pilsner up, "To new beginnings, then!"

"To new beginnings!"

⁂ Sydney stopped at her office and fumbled for her keys, while she tried not to pour hot chai all over herself. Brandon chose just that moment to come around the corner.

"Just in time!" He said, as he gingerly extricated the chai from her hand.

"Perfect," Sydney grinned, "Thanks."

"Let me get that for you, too." Brandon took her computer bag out of her hands, as well, and freed her hands completely.

"There they are!" Sydney said, as she finally located her keys.

She opened the door and took back her chai as Brandon followed her in and laid her bag on the desk.

He retrieved a stack of papers from his own messenger bag that hung from his shoulder. "Hey, do you have a moment to talk?"

"Yes, please. Welcome to my closet." Sydney gestured to a chair by her desk, happy at the unexpected, albeit temporary, reprieve from grading her last few papers before class.

Taking his seat, he grinned at her joke, "Your office isn't that bad. Kind of cozy, I'd say."

Sydney rolled her eyes at him remembering that same comment from the restaurant. "Nice try. Thanks."

"My pleasure." Brandon winked at her.

Ornery devil, she thought to herself.

"Here are Emily's papers back."

Sydney glanced up! Of course, the writings. She hadn't realized he'd read them all so quickly. She wasn't sure she was ready for any bad news. Last night had been the most fun she'd had in such a long time. She was still savoring it. But, this was important. Sobering, she braced herself.

"And.....?"

"Well, I'd like to say I don't think that there is a clear cut or immediate threat to Emily," Brandon began. "That being said, I think that the prudent thing to do is to see about finding her. I am mildly, but justifiably concerned on a few references to the finality of death. She refers to it as if it were something that she's seeing in the near future instead of the growing old and eventually dying kind of reference."

"So, is she suicidal?"

"I can't tell based on just the things she writes alone, but, since that's all I have, I'm only able to say I'm curious to find out more. I know it's important to your peace of mind, too. The main thing is, there's no indication of an immediate intent to do herself any harm. She appears to be very self-aware, actually. Just depressed. Maybe she's going through a rough time in life and venting on paper. Didn't you tell me that writing helped you deal with the problems in your failed marriage?"

Sydney nodded.

"Be that as it may, I want to remind you of two things. All I have to go off of is her writing, so I can't be sure. But, if she really wants to commit suicide, no one can stop her. Remember?"

"Yes, I know." Sydney didn't sound convincing even to her own ears, but she was working on it. It's like she knew it was true in her head, but her heart just wasn't sure.

"So my suggestion is that we see if we can figure out where she is and pay her a visit."

"Where do we start? The semester's already half over."

"Madge had her old school information. We could start there. Care to take a spring break trip? I already called, and their university is on spring break this week, so we're in luck. Their faculty will be back on campus Monday when our university goes on spring break, so we're not missing any classes."

Noting Sydney's hesitancy in answering, Brandon continued on, "Being the school counselor, perhaps I can get a few more questions answered than you can. My title lends weight without having to say anything specific."

Sydney thought for a moment. Surely they could find some answers, and it's not like they're heading off for a romantic getaway, she reasoned.

"What about Baxter and Bailey?" She definitely couldn't leave Baxter alone for even a couple of days. Voicing that opinion bought Sydney a little more time to come to terms with the idea. Was she really going to go away with this man? It still made her nervous, even knowing they'd be in separate hotel rooms.

Sensing impending victory, Brandon said, "I have a buddy who watches Bailey when I travel. He lives on a farm outside of town and, I'm sure he's got room for Baxter, too. I will call him today, but I'm sure he'll say yes."

"Well...." Sydney looked around her office as if searching for another excuse to hedge. "I'd have to look into making some arrangements, and we'll see."

"OK, you take care of the reservations, and let me know how much I owe ya. Fair enough?" Brandon tried not to smile too much or act too pleased that Sydney had somewhat said yes.

"Fair enough. If I've not found out anything more, or if she's not miraculously shown up in class, then we'll go. I'll make the arrangements, and we'll leave out 9 a.m. this coming Monday."

~ Sydney stood on her porch with her hands wrapped around her favorite steaming cup of tea, waiting for Brandon to return from dropping off "the boys," as he had started to call Bailey and Baxter.

The patchy snow that clung to the deep shadows of the forest had been steadily melting over the last few days as winter surrendered slowly to spring. Rising from the stubborn mounds of leftover snow peeked dark purple and sunshine yellow crocus. Here and there the anemone bloomed cherry red and bubble gum pink. New shoots of spring foliage had appeared as if overnight. The air seemed to have less of a bite to it, as well. Soon daffodils and tulips would be found around the countryside in vibrant clusters, and spring would take over in full force. Baxter and Bailey would no doubt be tickled to death to be out in the sunshine chasing rabbits while she and Brandon were away.

Sydney still couldn't believe she had agreed to the trip, but he had a point. A psychologist looking out for the welfare of a current student would get farther in questioning Emily's former teachers than she would— a teacher who was worried over a few essays. He can ask questions with implied urgency, but be protected by doctor-patient privilege if people got too nosey. She doubted she would get very far if she went alone. Secretly, even if she hadn't fully admitted it to herself, she really didn't want to be alone either.

With Baxter and Bailey squared away, and the bags tucked into the trunk, Sydney and Brandon headed out. Sydney drove this time. Being a passenger usually didn't sit well on her stomach, and she liked the feeling of being the one in control.

Control—that's funny. It'd been a long time since she'd felt in control of anything. It felt more like she had been running from something, rather than in control of it, and now it seemed she was running to something. Something she wasn't sure if she was going to like or not. Like or not, it had a purpose, though, and a sense of hope, rather than a sense of meaningless suffering. She felt, for once, the torment of losing David might have some good come out of it. She didn't like the idea that one of her students could be in trouble though.

In a way, she had David to thank for her heightened sensitivity to Emily's pain, and if it weren't for Emily and her essays, she'd not have been motivated into forming a friendship with Brandon either.

Friendship. Who was she trying to kid? She was beginning to realize just how much she was really starting to like Brandon's company. More than she'd like to admit. Definitely more than just friendship.

Sydney's thoughts had been more and more on Brandon and the what-if's of their current relationship and less and less on David and what could have been. Even thinking of David, saying his name inside her head, didn't send the familiar pang through her chest as it once had done. Granted, he'd always be inside her. There'd always be a tiny place for him in her heart that no one else could reach, but, more and more, her heart was making room for Brandon.

Sydney glanced over at Brandon. Ha! He was asleep. He had already dozed off in the car. Taking her eyes back off the road for a few seconds she allowed herself to admire him in repose. He *was* beautiful. She smiled to herself, and not for the first time in many weeks had she wondered what it'd be like to kiss him again. Really kiss him.

⁂ "Brandon. Bran....don." Sydney almost laughed at how deeply Brandon slept. "Brandon, we're here, wake up!" Oh, to be able to *sleep* like that!

Lying back in the seat, Brandon opened one eye and squinted at her. Sydney did laugh then. He looked like a surly little kid whose mom was trying unsuccessfully to get him up in time to catch the bus. She half expected him to request, "Ten more minutes, please." Impishly, she added, "It's time for school, let's go."

Yawning, Brandon stretched and rubbed the sleep out of his eyes. "Are we there already?" Returning his seat to the upright position, he saw the university and groaned. "You should have woke me up earlier and let me help drive."

"Nah, it was only a few hours, and apparently, you needed the sleep."

Sydney grabbed her purse, and they both got out of the car.

"This place is huge." Brandon noted, as he finger combed his hair and straightened his sleep disturbed clothes. "A lot bigger than our school."

"Yeah, it sure is."

Having found the main office, Brandon took the lead and began making inquiries about Emily. The information was not helpful. It was the same as they'd been told over the phone. Everyone who actually remembered her repeated the same thing—she was a small quiet girl with blonde hair who attended classes there until last fall. No other records were found besides the PO Box and the fact that she paid her tuition in cash. She was a liberal arts student. Not dissuaded, before they left the university Brandon made a few appointments to speak in person with a few of her teachers later that afternoon.

Sydney sighed as they got into the car. Checking her directions she headed in the direction of the hotel.

"It's not surprising with the office mainly manned by students that only a few remember her. I'm sure the turnover there is high for the student workers," Brandon offered reassuringly. "Maybe I'll have more luck when I meet with her former teachers this afternoon, after classes let out. There's a lot of information that we could find out from them that wouldn't be found in official records. Especially, since she attended class here in person. Don't let it get to you."

"I'm ok. Just a little tired." Sydney only partly fibbed. She needed to know Emily was OK.

Arriving at the Hilton, Sydney pulled into the circle drive. Brandon grabbed a baggage cart and unloaded the bags. Waiting with the luggage, Brandon watched Sydney pull away to park the car. He could tell she was worried. He was worried, too.

She'd come so far in the last few weeks. She was breaking out of her shell more and trusting him with her secrets. He knew no matter how far he'd come, that he still needed to take it slowly, especially now, as they delved deeper into Emily's situation. Every step in working with her to find Emily brought him that much closer to Sydney, but it also brought that much more of her past back to the surface. It was a tricky situation at best.

Sydney had made reservations for two separate rooms on the top floor. After checking in and receiving their room keys, they went their separate ways to unpack and freshen up. They agreed to meet for lunch in the hotel restaurant to discuss plans for the afternoon.

~ "I think it would be best if I go back alone this afternoon," Brandon began after they'd ordered lunch and the waitress left. "I'm concerned that, since you're not a psychologist, the teachers may hesitate to be completely honest with me if there's something they suspect. You don't mind, do you?"

Sydney nodded her head, "That makes sense. I didn't sleep much last night, and I think I'll take a nap. What time will you be back?"

"Five or six tonight. I'll call your cell when I'm on my way, and we'll meet for dinner."

Sydney thought that was a fine idea. They made plans to see each other later. After lunch Sydney retired to her room for that much needed nap.

It seemed she'd just fallen asleep when Brandon called a few minutes after 6pm. "Hey, gorgeous! You ready to eat?"

"Did you find out anything?"

"A little, but I'm starving. I'll tell you at dinner. Don't worry. It's not bad."

Sydney sighed, only mildly annoyed he wouldn't tell her over the phone. She'd slept hard, but instead of feeling refreshed she'd awakened groggy and irritable. She felt even more tired than before.

They met in the lobby and headed straight for the hotel restaurant again. Once seated they quickly ordered Beef, Chicken and Shrimp fajitas for two and a pair of Dos Equis to wash them down with.

"OK. No one had any definitive information on any mental health issues, but I did find one teacher who recalled that Emily worked at a local store—a little new and used bookstore called Second Story. I have the address here, and we can go after dinner—see what we can find out!"

"That's awesome! Our first breakthrough!" Sydney high-fived him. "How can you possibly be hungry with news like that!?"

"Well, there's no telling how long it'd be until I'd be able to eat if we went there first!" Brandon joked, and not half-heartedly either.

A lively sizzle announced the arrival of dinner. Sydney dug in with relish. Brandon was hoping her happiness wasn't short lived.

⁂ Pulling out the directions he'd printed off at the school, Brandon followed the instructions as he drove them from the hotel. The directions took them from the newer end of town to what looked like the original downtown main street, with its quaint brick buildings and diagonal parking spaces lining the sidewalk. Minutes later they arrived in front of a two story brick building—the "Second Story" signage was hand painted in yellow with black trim in big block letters across the large paned window. A "for sale or lease" sign hung on the front door.

"You've got to be kidding me!" Sydney cried in dismay.

"Well, that does suck, but there's a Realtor's phone number. It's not a dead end, yet."

He knew she was deeply frustrated. He wasn't terribly happy with the outcome either. It'd be nice to catch a break for a change.

Sydney nodded her head not trusting her voice with the angry tears that were threatening. Instead, she silently prayed for strength as she fished around in her purse for a pen.

"Hi, I'm calling about the store you have listed called Second Story."

Sydney looked up at Brandon. Just like him to keep a cool head. He's already taking care of it. Abandoning her search for the pen, Sydney just listened.

"Oh, you are? Yeah, we're here. We'll wait. Thanks."

"What?" Sydney asked.

"Her office is around the corner. The Realtor will be here in a few minutes."

A short while later, driving back to the hotel, Sydney and Brandon mulled over what they had discovered—as well as what they hadn't. They found out that the Realtor had been hired by an attorney representing the Halliwell family to take care of the sale of the property. If she wasn't able to sell it then they would consider a lease, the realtor dangled, trying to gauge their interest.

The lawyer wasn't forthcoming with how the property became available, a common question of buyers the Realtor confided, but she had heard the neighborhood gossip.

There was a young girl and her grandmother that ran the store. They both lived in the apartment above it. One night last fall, an ambulance came and took someone away, and the store never opened again. Weeks later the store was vacant and up for sale, but that's all she knew.

With that, they were back to square one, Sydney thought sullenly. All Brandon and she could do was hope and pray Emily showed up for class, or catch her coming to drop off her paper.

~ "I can't believe it's been another two weeks, April's almost over, and neither of us have been able to catch her dropping off her paper," complained Sydney, as she entered her office and plunked down in her chair. Brandon came in behind her and took the chair opposite the desk.

"The only times we haven't watched the door is very early, very late, and during our classes where we're teaching simultaneously," Brandon said. "You say the papers are dropped off in your drop box, right?"

"Yes."

"I'm sure we'll be able to catch her dropping them off then. We just need to expand our coverage. I have student workers. I'll assign them some work for the class, and I'll take the hours we teach at the same time."

"Perfect. She shouldn't be hard for one of us to spot then," agreed Sydney. "I plan to stay tonight and watch the door until the building closes, so that's covered for today. That means I won't be jogging tonight," Sydney said by way of an apology.

"That's ok, I have a late appointment with a client," Brandon replied. Checking his watch he rose to go. "Call me if she arrives."

"I will. See you tomorrow," said Sydney.

Brandon waved good-bye as he left.

The next day Sydney couldn't wait to see Brandon. "We're in luck," Sydney exclaimed. "Papers are due tomorrow, and I've checked and double checked. Her paper isn't in yet. You're covering the classes we both teach, and I can stay again tonight and then be here at 6 a.m. when doors open tomorrow." Sydney said, handing Brandon a copy of her schedule.

"Looks like we'll catch a break between now and then," Brandon said with a grin.

"I know. We will finally meet Emily!" Sydney was so excited.

Brandon smiled back.

"And thanks again for everything, Brandon."

"Any time, sweetie."

Morning seemed an eternity away. Emily hadn't been to her office the day before so it was a certainty that she'd have to drop the papers off in the morning. All night long Sydney had tossed and turned wondering what she'd say when Emily arrived. Standing in the hot shower she leaned her forehead to rest on the cool tile and tried to wake up. Of all days to be dead on her feet.

On autopilot she got dressed, all the while her mind was in high gear. How does one approach a stranger and ask if they're suicidal? Where would she start? How does she find out what's going on? What if Emily won't talk to her? The teachers that remembered her said she was shy.

If she won't talk how does she make sure to see her again? It's not like she can make her come to class. It's not like she can follow her and make her talk or lock her in her office for safe keeping. Stalking and imprisonment are both pretty much frowned upon regardless if someone has good intentions or not, Sydney thought wryly.

She grabbed her keys and headed out the door—her train of thought never derailed. She couldn't call the police or Emily's family either, for that matter. It's not like she or Brandon had anything solid to show the authorities, nor did they have any idea who her family was. Even if they did have the essay papers and showed them to the police, would they really act on them? If they did somehow get the police to act on them, what good would that do? If she didn't want help, it would pretty much alienate Emily from any help she and Brandon would have to offer if they jumped the gun like that.

Sydney mentally winced at her unfortunate choice of words.

No, she refused to believe they would be too late, even as she wondered how they would handle the situation once they found Emily.

Her faith in God had been badly shaken when David left—correction, when David had taken his own life. It was time to stop putting a softer face on the act. David didn't leave her. He didn't die of natural causes. He chose to pull a trigger. It wasn't her fault. It wasn't his friends or family's fault. It wasn't God's fault, either. She had prayed to God for forgiveness for blaming Him. She needed to forgive David, too. Sydney said a prayer again for His support in doing so.

Having picked up a dirty chai from Starbucks to help ease her way into the morning, Sydney decided to sit down the hall from her office door instead of inside with the door open, as she'd previously been doing. For some reason, she thought it important not to be inside her office when Emily dropped off her work. Emily had not made the effort to meet her in person and explain her lack of attendance, even though it wasn't required, so Sydney thought there might be a reason the drop offs occurred outside of her posted office hours.

Startled by the sound of a door opening behind her, Sydney turned expectantly to see Emily for the very first time. Instead, she found herself staring at Brandon, holding his own version of caffeine, and what looked like a box of donuts. Catching sight of her he grinned back like a kid in a candy store. "Dang, I thought I'd beat you and surprise you with these."

Sydney groaned, "You are way too happy to be up this early in the morning, counselor, and how on earth can you be hungry on top of it?"

Laughing at her sullen tone, Brandon sat down beside her.

"Someone's not a morning person!" he crooned to her.

Why do morning people always state the obvious, thought Sydney, as she mentally rolled her eyes? And in that sing-song voice, too?

Still smiling, Brandon pulled out a chocolate covered donut and began munching happily on it.

"Not normally, but especially not after a near sleepless night," Sydney grumped.

"Ah, I'm sorry. Worried about Emily?"

"Yeah, all night long. How can I not be worried? I'm not sure what to do once I see her. What do I say? How do I start?"

"'Hello' usually works for me." Brandon joked, and was rewarded with a none-too-gentle elbow in his side. "Try not to worry. We'll figure something out."

"Donut?" Brandon smiled at her while holding the open box of donuts. "There's sausage rolls in there, too. I wasn't sure what you'd be in the mood for, so I bought a variety."

Despite herself, Sydney found she did have something of an appetite and chose a sausage roll. Taking a bite she was thrilled to find it filled with cheese, too!

"Thanks, that was thoughtful of you," she said around a mouthful of yummy deliciousness. "I didn't expect you to be here, though."

"Are you kidding me? I wouldn't let you face this alone." He winked at her then. Sydney rolled her eyes for real this time, all the while grinning. Seriously. He was such a big kid.

Sobering, Brandon answered, "I really want to be there for you Sydney—every time you need me. When you're ready, that is."

Sydney looked at him again. She knew what he meant. He wanted to be with her past this adventure with Emily. To be with her as more than friends. She wouldn't be alone anymore.

Not alone. Could it be real? How wonderful it would be to think in terms of not being alone anymore. Was she really ready for that? Yeah, she thought. She could get used to that.

Sydney opened her mouth to tell him just that, when the door opened again, and she and Brandon turned in unison to look. Disappointment quickly set in when a young man in a grey uniform strolled in rather than a small blonde girl.

They watched as the delivery man walked to Sydney's door, insert an envelope, and then turn to leave.

Sydney got up thinking she'd just received an early mail call, but as she reached her drop box, she realized the envelope was the same style that all of Emily's papers came in. Wait a minute! Mail was delivered to the campus post office by the U.S. Postal Service. After that, it's sorted by campus personnel, and student couriers ferry the mail out to the teachers. This was a *personal* delivery, not a normal university mail drop.

She jerked the envelope out of the holder. Her name was handwritten on the front, just like all the others. What was going on here!? Emily wasn't a man. Was she?

"Wait!" she shouted.

Upon hearing Sydney's shout, Brandon sprung out of his seat and headed toward the exit.

"Wait, sir, I need to speak with you for a moment." Sydney rushed to catch up with the courier.

Brandon blocked the door, effectively closing off the delivery man's retreat.

Clearly bewildered, and feeling a little uneasy at Brandon's rather large and determined presence, the man stopped halfway and turned. He looked warily back and forth from Sydney to Brandon. Sydney jogged to catch up with the delivery man, waving the envelope in her hand.

"I'm Sydney Mackenzie, the professor whose office you've been delivering these to. I'm sorry to startle you, but we need to ask you a question. Do you know Emily Halliwell? I really need to find her."

"No. I don't. I just pick these up and deliver them." The delivery man said.

"Where? Where do you pick them up from?" Brandon asked, as he took a less menacing position away from the door.

"Fairview. Fairview Nursing Home," said the man as he backed toward the door. "I just pick them up at the front desk."

"What's the name on the invoice," Brandon said, thinking quickly.

The young man checked his digital read out. "Paid for by a Claire E. Halliwell. I have to go. I've got lots to do today," and, with that, he bolted out the door.

"Nursing home?" Sydney was bewildered. "Why would a 25 year old girl be in a nursing home? And I thought her name was Emily, not Claire."

"What did Madge say her middle name was?"

"She didn't register with one. Just Emily Halliwell," said Sydney.

"Well, maybe she's Claire Emily Halliwell. There's only one way to find out," Brandon said. "We'll go this afternoon, after our classes let out. I'll drive."

≈ The day couldn't go any slower for Sydney short of time stopping altogether, although several times she checked the clock just to make sure it hadn't. Her morning tutoring hours and regularly scheduled classes crawled by. Inch worms travel faster than this, she thought to herself.

She was having trouble concentrating on her lessons, not even hearing students when they asked her a question. She hadn't been able to eat at lunch either, although Brandon dropped in at 11 to see if she wanted to go to the cafeteria with him. She'd brought her lunch, she told him. It sat unopened in her mini-fridge hours later.

They could leave at 3 o'clock, but at 1:47 it seemed like an eternity until then. Time was creeping by as her mind hashed and rehashed what she knew and didn't know about Emily.

She was obviously alive as of yesterday when the courier picked up the envelope, so that was something. Even Brandon said she wasn't necessarily in any danger from what he could tell. They were only trying to find her to ascertain her true mental state. Depression doesn't kill. Not as a general rule, and the writing could all be just the emotional outlet of a person having a hard time in life. That's all.

Sometimes, she sounded so hopeless, so alone. David had only been emotionally isolated—by choice. He'd had friends and family, and he hadn't chosen to turn to any of them. Emily wrote about being alone. At least Sydney could make sure Emily knew she was there if she needed her. Make sure Emily knew she wasn't alone. Just in case. It was the least she could do. Wasn't it?

Seriously! The waiting was killing her, but, it's not like she could cancel classes and go off on what could very well be a wild goose chase, she reasoned. She had a job to do, and the other students that needed her attention.

On top of that, this recent essay of Emily's sounded positive. The writing topic was if you could be anything in the world, career-wise, what would it be? What would be your magnum opus in that profession? She wanted her students to dream big—to visualize they could do anything they put their mind to.

Sydney had already read Emily's paper and searched for clues as to her current mental state. There was no drama this time. No dark depressing revelations. Emily would be a doctor. Many of her students chose lofty professions, like being a doctor or lawyer, with aspirations of saving peoples' lives or liberating the oppressed and wrongfully accused. A few chose more fantastic careers like being an all-star NFL quarterback and making the winning touchdown, a famous movie star winning an Oscar, or the next American Idol contestant winning a million dollars. These were the fun kind of essays to read.

Maybe she'd been over-exaggerating Emily's earlier essays. Maybe this was just some melodramatic girl and the whole thing was some sort of drama queen seeking attention. That didn't make complete sense though. Didn't a drama queen crave the public stage and an audience to react to? She didn't know, but that's why she'd approached Brandon, and he didn't readily dismiss it as such. So she didn't feel like she was totally imagining things.

Sydney's mind drifted back to the mystery of the nursing home. Why were the papers being picked up at a nursing home? Did she live there? That wouldn't make sense for a young girl to be in an assisted living facility unless she was a patient. If that were the case, then she definitely had no family to live with or to even pick up and deliver her essays.

Had she already attempted suicide, but failed? What was it that Brandon had told her about women and suicide? They're not as successful, but try three times more often than men? Was Emily somehow physically incapacitated and in need of the type of care a nursing home provided? Is that why she intimated an end being near— because she was going to try again? Or that she'd tried and damaged herself so thoroughly that she was on the verge of death?

That didn't quite make sense either. She couldn't be too incapacitated. She could still type out her work.

Work! Or maybe, Emily worked at the nursing home. If she works there, maybe it was just more convenient to drop off her work for pickup and delivery from her job instead of her home, especially, if she worked nights and slept days. Maybe that's why she didn't bring the essays to school *personally*! She could be sleeping.

Maybe the delivery place wouldn't pick up from a PO Box either. If she rented a house or an apartment somewhere, she might prefer to receive her mail at a secure location such as a PO Box, rather than at another person's residence. That also made sense, if she was renting a place with several other college students. So she might use her office as a pick up location for her homework instead.

An interest in being a doctor would be right along the lines of someone already working in the medical profession. Except, her degree was in liberal arts. Well, it wouldn't be the first time a student gained one degree, and then decided they wanted to be something else and start over in school. She had. So had Brandon.

Or maybe she knew someone who died of cancer—a loved one perhaps. Maybe their death is why she's interested in becoming a doctor. Maybe that's why she's depressed.

She still didn't understand, though—why pay the expense of a delivery service and not just utilize the good ole' United States Postal Service? To gain reliable on-time delivery? Mentally throwing up her hands, Sydney realized this particular train of thought was leading nowhere, too.

Exasperated, she glanced at the clock again. 1:55 p.m. One more class, and they could leave for Fairview.

⁓ Before they left for the nursing home, Brandon brought Bailey over. He would keep Baxter company in Sydney's backyard while they were away. After the boys were settled, Brandon handed the directions to Fairview to Sydney as they headed out.

"You get to be the navigator this time," he joked.

"Thanks, Brandon," said Sydney, hoping she didn't get car sick. She didn't complain. She was too distressed and distracted to drive safely anyway.

Other than the occasional need to clarify directions, neither spoke on the way to the nursing home, each keeping company with their own thoughts.

Fairview was in a nearby suburb, less than an hour from the college via the interstate. The metal power poles laden with half a dozen lines marched up and down the expressway, eventually giving way to simple wooden poles with twin lines, as the four-way interstate narrowed to a two-lane country highway.

Taking the highway made the trip both fast and peaceful. The road meandered through various farmers' fields dotted with the intermittent cluster of trees. Rectangular shapes of early green crops broke up the brown dead grasslands still dotted with the occasional shaded patch of snow. Here and there Sydney could see small herds of cows grazing in a pasture. The renewal of life was as evident in the tender green crops as it was in the wobbly calves playing at their mothers' feet.

More of the same played out over the course of the drive. The sameness of scenery prompted Sydney's thoughts to turn inward. What would they find at the nursing home? Would finding the worst be better than not knowing? Probably, but as Sydney replayed the past weeks over and over one thought became clearer. Brandon was the future, and whatever happened today or tomorrow, Emily wasn't. Oh, she'd help her as she'd help anyone else who battled this burden. She'd do right by her time with David, but he was the past. Brandon, well, she felt hope for the future.

The nursing home was located just off the highway. It looked more like a resort than an elderly convalescence facility. Three stories tall, it was all white and boasted numerous rooms, each with its own large picture window. On either end, there were exterior staircases with wheel chair lifts.

The front driveway turned in a wide arc before the main entrance. A row of dwarf Alberta Spruce dotted the driveway from one end to the other, each sporting new lime green growth. A wide covered patio protected visitors from the elements and shaded the benches near the door from the sun. Off behind the main building, a number of individual cottages clustered together for residents who needed less care than the others and who craved a bit more independence. The lawn was beautifully manicured, looking more like a golf course without the flags and holes than an assisted living facility. Flower beds adorned the front sidewalk that stretched from one end of the building to the other. Here and there spring flowers were just starting to bloom.

In front of the main oval was a small parking lot with a sign welcoming guests to "park here." Brandon turned in and parked the car.

Sydney opened the car door and stood staring up at the nursing home, one foot on the pavement, and one still in the car. It was as if she instinctively knew they were approaching a truth which, once discovered, there was no turning back from. Her body held her back a moment before taking the final step—as if a part of her clung to the past and was unable to commit to the future.

Brandon rounded the car and held out his hand to her.

She looked at it, uncertainly. Raising her eyes, she looked into his. There she found an anchor. Although, she was certain no horror would be found in a blood soaked carpet, she still feared the unexpected, but whatever awaited her, this time she wouldn't be alone. No matter what they found, she would have Brandon with her.

While her heart hammered with uncertainty, his eyes evinced a peace that they would be able to handle it together. If Emily was in trouble in there, they would both be there to help. If she'd let them.

As if speaking to her thoughts aloud, Brandon said, "No matter what, we're going to face this together. It's going to be all right."

She nodded mutely, removed her foot from the car. She stood tall as she resolutely shut the door. Hand in hand they walked up the stairs and into Fairview.

Approaching the front desk, Sydney was disappointed to find none of the women working had blonde hair, but then again, she could be working nights, or changed her hair color. Her mind was chasing all possibilities at once.

"Good Afternoon miss, we're looking for Miss. Claire E. Halliwell," Brandon announced.

The young lady looked up and pointed to a book and a pen. "Please sign in. Ms. Halliwell doesn't get many visitors. Are you family?" The receptionist eyed them curiously.

"No, but we're friends of the family, you might say."

"Well, she'll be happy to have some company. Please wait here while I announce your arrival and see if she is up to seeing you." She left them waiting as she headed down the corridor.

Sydney looked around. It didn't appear Emily worked here. The nurse spoke as if she was a patient instead of an employee, and if by chance it was the latter, she certainly didn't work nights if she was available to be seen during the day.

Sydney felt sick.

The receptionist returned and announced that Ms. Halliwell had just come out of a minor procedure. She was still a little groggy from the anesthesia, however, she said she felt she was up to seeing them.

"I can tell she's excited to have company, but please, only stay a moment. She is more out of it than she realizes. If you can, please say hello, and then tell her you'll come spend more time with her shortly. She'll be more alert in an hour or so," gesturing them to follow her, she turned and led them down the hall.

Sydney and Bandon agreed as they followed her to a room.

"Ms. Claire...are you awake, Ms. Claire?" The receptionist placed her hand on the frail small-boned hand of an old woman, not a young girl. Her hair was sparkling white, all fine and wispy. It was drawn back into a little bun on the top of her head. Her bun looked like a fluffy birds nest. She had pale, almost translucent skin and was so petite she looked like a tiny porcelain doll. Her eyes fluttered open— a beautiful slate blue.

"Emily, is that you?" she murmured.

"It's Lilly, Ms. Claire. Are you sure you're awake enough to have some company?" Lilly gently inquired.

"That's fine, that's fine," whispered Ms. Claire.

"I'll be down the hall if you need me," Lilly said, and she left them to their visit.

Brandon and Sydney drew closer, unsure if Ms. Claire was actually awake. Sydney took in her surroundings and spotted a picture on the nightstand of a beautiful blonde headed girl. She pointed it out to Brandon. He nodded in return.

"Who is it?" Ms. Claire asked, finally opening her eyes a little.

"Ms. Claire, my name is Brandon, and this is Sydney," Brandon began, "we're teachers at the school where Emily is enrolled, and we're looking for her."

"Emily? My grandbaby isn't here. Such a sweet child. " Claire smiled and closed her eyes again.

"Ms. Claire, can you tell us where to find Emily? We would like to see her," Sydney replied.

Silence met her words.

"Ms. Claire?"

Ms. Claire appeared to be sleeping.

Brandon walked to her bedside and gently placed his hand on top of hers. Her eyes fluttered again then closed. She smiled at his touch.

"Ms. Claire, can you tell us where to find Emily, please?"

Ms. Claire's eyes opened just a bit.

"Emily? Where's Emily? Oh, she's at 1109 Emerald Lane—K17," her voice drifted off as her eyes closed again.

Sydney grinned in triumph! Finally, they had an address!

"Thank you, Ms. Claire," Brandon said, as he patted her hand. Brandon took a moment and tucked her blanket in around her shoulders before slipping quietly out of the room with Sydney.

"We're on eleventh street," noted Brandon. "Her apartment should be near here," he said, as they retraced their steps back to the entrance.

Sydney nodded, too excited for words. This was it. An address!

On their way out Brandon asked a nurse rushing by, "Excuse me, please. Could you tell us where we can find 1109 Emerald Lane?"

"Yeah. Take a right at the end of the main drive. We're on eleventh Street. Then go seven blocks to Emerald Lane, and take a right again. You'll be on eleventh and Emerald." She returned as she hurried off.

"Thanks." Brandon called after her.

"Let's go."

Brandon walked Sydney to the car and opened the passenger door for her. Hurrying to the other side, he climbed into the driver's seat, started the car, buckled up, and took her hand. He gave her a meaningful glance as if to say, "This is it." She smiled and squeezed his hand in reply.

Sydney rode along in silence with a mind full of thoughts. This was it. She was about to meet the girl who had become almost a friend over the last fourteen weeks of class—kind of like a pen pal, sort of. She had given Sydney a gift in letting her see into a world David must have known all along, but had never shared. She was so thankful for Emily's willingness to let others glimpse inside her personal journey. And she was about to meet her in person for the first time, but not really meet her for the first time, for they'd kind of already met through her work. It was Emily who would be meeting Sydney for the first time. For Sydney, Emily was neither stranger nor friend, but in some ways she knew her more than most people who had known each other for years. It was an odd sort of intimacy with a stranger.

All this time, Brandon and she had searched for her and now at the moment of truth, Sydney still had no idea what she was going to say. One couldn't just barge in and blurt out, are you going to kill yourself? Geez, how do you do this delicately? Sydney was glad Brandon was with her. She hoped if her own wits were to fail her that he would know what to do. If not, she prayed God would help them both.

A short time later they rounded the curve and turned onto Emerald Lane. Sydney eagerly looked at the landscaped scenery. They were passing a cemetery. Cherubs sat on a tombstone as if standing sentinel to a doorway. Crosses stood tall, marking hallowed ground. Sydney looked ahead trying to see the apartment complex. K17, wasn't it? All she saw was the cemetery. It's probably over the rise, she guessed, but as they crested the hill, the cemetery opened up below into a cul-de-sac at the end of the drive. Other than a small chapel at the end, there was nothing to see except a green expanse of manicured lawn lined with dark marble and sun-bleached tombstones. No apartment complex.

"This doesn't make any sense. You don't think she works here, do you?" asked Sydney.

"Not the best job choice for someone that's depressed, maybe," answered Brandon.

"Do you think we we got the address wrong?"

Ahead was a small stucco chapel with a wooden cross perched high atop the steeple. The windows were stained glass and covered in beautiful iron filigree. The chapel was encircled with a tiny iron picket fence with a little gate in the front. Driving up to it, they both looked for an address number.

"1109 Emerald Lane," Brandon read off.

"So this *is* the place. Maybe she's a caretaker? Or do you think the woman is completely senile?" asked Sydney.

"No, she didn't seem senile, just sleepy. I think they'd have warned us if she were senile, but this is definitely strange. I doubt this is where the caretaker works. That chapel looks more like where one would hold a small graveside service than a caretaker's office. Damn. This is obviously the wrong address. Let's just go back and see if she is more awake. Perhaps she has more family nearby we can talk to."

Brandon began to turn the car around when Sydney gasped, "Oh, my God, no."

He looked in the direction of Sydney's gaze and saw the small placards then. The cemetery was divided into sections by letters of the alphabet.

"It can't be." Sydney breathed.

Understanding the direction of her thoughts, Brandon replied, "We need to know, let's go."

They parked the car and got out. Sydney took Brandon's hand. Memories of David's funeral surfaced. Sad faces staring back at her with questions in their eyes. How could she not have known? Was she to blame? Did she drive him to it? She had felt the stinging accusations in every stare.

She saw his casket—closed for the ceremony. It was baby blue. A color she and his mom picked out to compliment his eyes that were closed forever.

Stop it, Sydney, she ordered herself. His funeral was over. God is merciful, and David had once said he was a believer. If so, he was in paradise. He was whole and well and loved.

She pushed the ghosts back to the past. It was where they belonged. She had to concentrate on the now.

They passed the lettered sections one by one. Each plot in that section had a number. They found section K and began counting till they reached number 17.

Here lies our beloved daughter and granddaughter,

Emily Frances Halliwell

Born December 25th....

Died....

Sydney fell to her knees. Died....

"Brandon, she died last fall. She died before class ever started. She's not going to commit suicide. She's not just committed suicide. She's already dead. Damn it, Brandon she's already dead. We're too late. But how? Why?"

They were too late. Emily would never know how much she helped others with her writings. She would never know how much she'd helped Sydney finally begin to heal from David's death. How much her open and honest essays had provided her with a little insight into the world of depression. How her words offered the wisdom Sydney needed that only a survivor of depression could impart. Sydney wouldn't be able to tell her what a gifted writer she was. That her grades were good and that she was going to graduate. Oh, God, they were too late.

Tears fell furiously on her face as Sydney wrestled with the host of emotions. Brandon sat down behind her and held her while she took it all in—let it all out.

Sydney was angry that she was dead and desperately saddened that Emily was gone. She grieved for this young girl who was now a part of their lives and who would never be known deeper. How could she be too late? How could she be too late when she didn't even know the girl when it happened? Why didn't anyone stop her then? Who let Emily down?

"We're going back." Sydney declared. She had to have answers. She had a right to know. She stood and wiped away the tears. "Someone has the answers, and we're going to find them."

Brandon got up, and looked at her uncertainly. "Are you sure?"

"Yes, I'm sure."

Sydney was determined to find out the truth. She had known this time. She had tried to help. Someone had the answers. And she was going to find out what had happened.

They drove back to the nursing home. Walking in, they found the nurse that had given them directions.

"Excuse me," Sydney started.

"Oh, did you get lost?"

"No, we found it... does she know," motioning toward Emily's grandmother's room, "Does she understand that Emily is dead?"

"I'm sorry, but didn't you know that, too?" Realizing the truth by their expressions, she rushed to say, "Lord above, I'm so sorry. I thought you knew. That must have been quite a shock to you both. I'm so terribly sorry."

"I'm confused. Why does she talk about her granddaughter as if she's alive? Why send us there like that?" Sydney's hurt resounded in the unspoken accusation.

"I'm sorry, ma'am. Ms. Claire doesn't speak of Emily as if she is dead and gone. Ms. Claire is a born and bred Southern Baptist.

To her, Emily isn't dead. She's is in heaven, and she believes her granddaughter is looking down on us all right now. Ms. Claire even talks to her as if she were in the room sometimes."

"So she's not crazy?" Brandon inquired.

"Heaven's no, Ms. Clair is a little eccentric, and sometimes when she's tired she gets confused and forgets things, but she's all there. Why don't you go talk to her? She's more alert now that the anesthetic has worn off, and I'm sure she'd love to tell you all about her. Emily was all she had, so she doesn't get many visitors anymore. She gets very lonely."

"That's a good idea, thank you," Brandon said, graciously. He took Sydney's hand and headed for Ms. Claire's room.

Sydney wasn't sure she wanted to go, but she couldn't stop now.

Brandon and Sydney walked through the TV room, past the nurses' lounge, back to Claire's private room.

"You're back." She said as they entered. "Did you talk to her?" Claire asked, excitedly.

She was clearly more lucid and out of bed now, sitting up in her wheel chair. Her eyes were bright and shining. She resembled a fluttery little bird—fragile nonetheless. From her upright position they could tell she was gently bent and stooped from the ravages of time. Her smile welcomed them warmly, as she gestured toward nearby chairs.

Sydney and Brandon sat down.

Sydney began, "Yes, but, well. Pardon us, Ms. Claire. My name is Sydney, I teach the creative writing class that Emily's enrolled in. This is Brandon. He works at the school, too. We came to see her, but we didn't realize Emily was dead, so this is quite a shock to us."

"Emily's in heaven, sweet child. She's able to hear you though. She'll be happy that you visited her."

Sydney took a deep breath and prayed for patience and strength. How did it happen? She needed to know. How did Emily die? Was it like David? She didn't want to know, but she knew she couldn't find the closure she had to have any other way. They'd been on this journey too long, and now that they were here, she couldn't let it end—not until they knew it all.

Brandon edged his chair closer to Sydney, reached over and took her hand. Sydney looked into his eyes trying to communicate her thoughts. He smiled, and nodded his head encouragingly. She needed to exorcize her ghosts. He wasn't going to do it for her. He loved her that much to let her ask the question herself.

Swallowing, Sydney nodded back. Her voice shook, but she spoke clearly, "Ms. Claire, how did Emily die?"

Ms. Claire smiled a sad smile then. "Emily had the cancer, and they couldn't make it go away, the poor child."

"So cancer is how she died?"

"Yes, and she was a brave one, too."

Sydney felt light-headed. She didn't kill herself. She wasn't too late!

"When she was diagnosed, they said surgery wasn't possible," Claire continued. "That they'd try chemo and drugs—nasty stuff made her sick more often than not. Sucked the life right out of her, it did. Those doctors never did give her much hope anyhow. They said the treatment was just buying her time. She fought that cancer long enough to keep her promise, though."

"Promise?" asked Sydney, her brow furrowed in confusion.

"What promise?" Brandon echoed. He briefly squeezed Sydney's hand again and smiled his reassurances. Sydney half expected him to wink at her and couldn't help but weakly smile back.

"Well..." Ms. Claire began, as she adjusted her dress and scooted back in her chair—settling in, as if to tell a bedtime story to a child. "Emily's parents died when she was in her senior year of high school. In fact, she was with them both when it happened."

Brandon and Sydney glanced at each other. They both knew what it was like losing someone you loved—the devastation. Poor Emily, losing both her parents. And then Claire? It was hard to imagine losing your child and grandchild, too.

"They were driving home one night from dinner. Emily was a senior, and she'd been accepted to college, you see. Steak and shrimp was always Emily's favorite thing to eat. They had been out celebrating at some fancy place, and they were headed back home."

"Her daddy never saw the deer until it was too late and, bless his soul, he swerved to miss it. My boy always did have a soft spot for animals. They say he lost control of the car. When it hit the ditch, it flipped and rolled."

Ms. Claire fell silent and stared off in the distance, seeing the scene in her mind. Tears welled in her eyes and spilled over, making slow tracks down her freshly powdered cheeks. Sydney and Brandon waited patiently as they imagined the scene themselves. Ms. Claire remembered herself, and glanced back at Sydney and Brandon. Dabbing her eyes she returned her gaze to the distance, drew a deep breath and continued.

"Emily's father died within minutes of the wreck. He lived long enough to tell her he was proud of her. How much he loved her and her mother. Emily was daddy's little girl."

"Her mother lived a little longer. No girl was ever closer to her mother than Emily. They were thick as thieves, those two. More like best friends than parent and child. As Emily held her momma in her arms she made Emily promise. Promise that she would go to school and finish college."

Ms. Claire looked at both of them then.

"You see, we come from modest means. Ha! Modest means is the fancy way to say we was poor folk. My momma, she grew up on a farm with dirt floors to live on, all three sisters sharing a bed, and well water to drink. She inherited the farm after her parents passed, such as it was."

"Me? I grew up on the same farm—well, not exactly the same. The remodeled house did have floors," chuckled Ms. Claire. "I never did finish my high schoolin'. Momma needed me to help with the babies and keep the house while she worked the fields with daddy. I made sure my baby boy finished high school, though."

"Our Emily, now she was our pride and joy. She was the only one in our family to ever make it. She was the first one that not only finished high school—and with honors at that, I don't mind telling you—but she had a chance to go to college, too. She'd earned herself one of those academic scholarships. Her parents made her make that promise to go to college. Not only go, mind you, but to finish. They knew they couldn't be there to help her and that it'd be hard. Hard losing them. Hard to finish growin' up without parents. Hard to go to school. And hard to make a living without a degree. They knew if she made that promise she'd keep it. She loved her parents that much. She wouldn't break that promise—not my girl."

"She came to live with me then and helped me in our little store," Ms. Claire continued on, reminding them the story hadn't ended. It had only just begun. "I hadn't been able to keep the farm so I sold it, and I bought a little bookstore that had an apartment up the stairs. She was a great help to me taking care of that store."

"She enrolled in school, too. Just like she said she would. Her parents left her well enough off through their life insurance policies that she could go to school like she planned. She even refused the scholarships she'd earned. Darling girl said she'd use her inheritance and leave the scholarship to someone who *really* needed it."

Ms. Clair laughed at that. "That girl was somethin' else."

"Then they found the cancer. She fought hard. Fought it while going to school. Pert' near wore her out, though, but she kept on fighting."

"Finally, the doctors told her they couldn't do any more, and she knew she had to make the decision to quit the chemo. To make her peace with the world. Her time had run out. Problem was, Emily was one class shy of graduating."

"I remember the day she came home chattering like a magpie, she was. She was so wound up, I barely made sense of what she was saying. I was amazed to see her so excited. The cancer, you see, had worn her down so much she was dead on her feet most of the time, but that day, her eyes were sparkling, and she was back to her old self again."

"She said she heard about your class from a friend who'd transferred to her college from the one you're at, and she had found the answer. She enrolled in your class and got to work. Those last week's she wrote all them assignments out one by one. I've never seen her so determined. Sometimes it seemed," Ms. Claire said, almost to herself, "as if she was pouring her very soul into those writings—emptying out all her pain and fears onto paper. Getting ready to say good-bye to the world, I guess she was. She'd already made her peace with the Almighty."

Ms. Claire looked at them with guilt in her eyes. With an almost pleading note in her voice she confessed, "I sent them in for her. I's afraid if y'all knew, you'd not let her graduate." Another single tear followed the first.

With a tremor in her voice Ms. Claire asked, "She'll graduate.... won't she?"

Brandon and Sydney looked at each other and smiled. A singular determination showed on their faces as they turned in unison to Ms. Claire and said "yes," at the very same time.

~ Sydney glanced at Brandon on the drive home. That kind of love—was it possible? In a moment she realized she already knew the answer. Emily had found a way to keep a promise made out of love for another. A promise she kept even in death. What impossible odds Emily had overcome—the death of both her parents, both!—In her arms, on the night that they were out celebrating *her* graduating high school and *her* getting accepted into college. Had Emily felt guilty? Blamed herself for her success contributing to her parent's death? If they'd not been out celebrating because Emily was going to college, they'd be alive today, maybe. If only they'd stayed home, like Sydney said to herself about her conference—her success, her loved one, her fault. She saw anew how wrong she'd been to blame herself.

Then being diagnosed with cancer. That alone would devastate most people and make them want to quit—quit living, let alone college! Emily fought her long fight with cancer, all while going to college—a task that many normal young people often failed at. When it looked like the cancer would win, Emily still found a way. Love found a way.

And that kind of love existed. It was right in front of her now. She loved Brandon. Why she hadn't wanted to see that before, she didn't know. Sydney knew now, in that very moment, that love—their love—would find a way.

~Epilogue~

~ Graduation day dawned cloudy with thunderstorms growing in the distance. Everyone in the outdoor assembly prayed hard that the summer showers would hold off long enough for the ceremony.

The students filed in quickly as the pomp and circumstance played. Honor students and valedictorians gave speeches—some punctuated with jokes and others spoken through tears. Special presentations and awards were given. Prayers for the future were said.

And then that precious moment began—when the students stood, in all their finery, and began the final leg of their journey from college student to college graduate. This was it. The culmination of years of hard work and late nights—of hard won triumphs and hard to swallow failures, but success was theirs, at last! Each walked proudly across the stage as their name was called across the loud speaker. Happy tears of joy, and in some cases relief, coursed down the cheeks of parents in the stands. Grandparents beamed proudly—but none prouder than Claire Halliwell.

Ms. Claire sat quietly at the back of the stage in her wheelchair watching the happy students rejoice as they walked by. Her face glowed as bright as the white nimbus of her hair, as she took in every moment of their joy. A beautiful corsage rose and fell proudly on her breast—a thoughtful gift from Brandon to accent her special day. When the time came, an honor student rolled her forward, with her tiny trembling hands outstretched, to receive by proxy the diploma for Emily Frances Halliwell—posthumous graduate.

By graduation day, every student at the University knew of Emily's courage and of her passing. When her name was called,

Emily was honored with a booming standing ovation. The whole ceremony paused to celebrate Emily's finest achievement. Claire wept tears of joy that only made her smile that much more beautiful, as she waved thank you to the students paying homage to her granddaughter and fiercely clutched the diploma tightly to her chest with her other hand.

The ceremony ended with as much joy as it began. The students had just tossed their caps into the sky when the random warning drops of rain began to fall, reminding them all that the storm wasn't going to be patient for long. Friends hugged each other quickly as families headed for the shelter of their cars before the rain could set in.

Brandon took Ms. Claire to the lift that would take her back to the senior center. They'd be visiting soon, he assured her. The "boys" would come, too, he promised. Ms. Claire was family now.

Birds called back and forth as the families departed. Songbirds serenaded a new generation moving on with their future. Sydney recalled someone once told her that birds sing in the voice of lost lovers. Or was it with the voices of the dead? All she heard now was a song of hope.

Brandon came up behind her then. He wrapped his arms around her and handed her a folded up piece of paper. Sydney craned her neck and looked at him, "What's this?"

"Read it," he said. "Ms. Claire wanted you to have it."

Sydney opened up the letter.

Dear Grandma,

Thank you so much for everything. I know the end is coming soon and you hate to see me suffer, but know that I'm going to be OK. I will be in heaven with momma and daddy, and we'll be waiting for you.

I know this has been so hard on you. I thought about ending it so many times so I could spare you the pain of seeing me slowly get sicker and eventually die, but I just couldn't. I knew through all the pain and depressing times that there had to be a reason for my suffering. That God would somehow use this for good. I haven't figured out if I'm right, or how He'll work that out, but, then again, I may never know—and that's OK, too.

Until we meet again, grandma.

Love you bunches,

Emily

~About the Author~

This is the first novel by author Karen Marie Graham. As a wife, mother of four and step-mother of two, she spends most of her time with her family. With what's left over, she can be found gardening, playing with pets, reading, writing and at the occasional Dave Matthews Band concert. She also has two more books in the works.

Please email her at *karenmariegraham@gmail.com* to share your feedback. She'd love to hear from you!

Visit us at: *www.Books-A-Daisy.com*

http://books-a-daisy.com/authors/karen-marie-graham

Facebook.com/BooksADaisy

Facebook.com/ThePromisesYouKeep

@karenmarieg1

@PromisesYouKeep

Pinterest.com/BooksADaisy

http://www.amazon.com/Karen-Marie-Graham/e/B008ED92AO/

Note from the author: *Thank you, so much, for your purchase of this book. I hope you enjoyed Sydney and Emily's story. I'd be so honored if you'd leave feedback and share your thoughts with other readers on Amazon.com and GoodReads. Authors appreciate reviews more than you know. And thanks again for reading!*

Made in the USA
Charleston, SC
11 April 2015